Steel Soldier

Rusted Wasteland
Book 5

Cameron Coral

Copyright © 2023 by Cameron Coral

Edited by Lori Diederich

Cover by Roy Migabon

9 8 7 6 5 4 3 2 1

2nd edition, March 2024

Stay updated on Cameron's books by signing up for the Cameron Coral Reading List:
CameronCoral.com/sign-up

You'll be added to my reading list, and I'll send you a digital copy of *CROSSING THE VOID: A Space Opera Science-Fiction Short Story* to say thank you.

Contents

Chapter 1
Chase

Shadow and the pack were forty-three miles outside of Cleveland when Var picked up the heat signature traces of something organic. Something big. The Rovers' hydraulic-powered, precision-crafted steel legs had pumped past plenty of deer and feral dogs as they raced across abandoned highways littered with rusting cars and through a Midwest countryside long overgrown with invasive vines and weeds. Whatever creature Var sensed lacked the muscular density of a deer and was a lot slower than an organic canine.

Shadow followed and obeyed. She knew her place was beta, or second-in-command, and things worked better that way. Built a year after her, Var had a stronger, impenetrable new hull, so he was the obvious choice to be pack leader and fulfill Mach X's orders. The human children had been abducted from inside their Manhattan tower. *Home.* Shadow's favorite place in the whole world. She'd found the situation almost impossible to compute—a NannyBot had gone rogue, joined with enemies to fight off the pack, and escaped in an autonomous semi-truck. The pack had chased the zero-emission rig halfway across the country, tracking its electromagnetic radiation.

But something strange had happened on their journey. Their master had always been inside their intralink, commanding them, watching them, seeing and even experiencing what the Rovers did. Shadow's circuitry hummed when Master praised her. But when he'd been angry—the two times she'd done something wrong—it had been the worst time Shadow could remember.

So, it was strange that after the skirmish in Manhattan, no follow-up orders had been sent. For Shadow, it was downright unpleasant not to sense Master's presence. Perhaps he was too busy forming a plan to attack the enemies. Shadow didn't ask Var, and neither did Raze or Fang, even though they all felt Master's void. Shadow obeyed Var as he executed their last known orders, a mission that was crystal clear—destroy the NannyBot and retrieve the children.

Var slowed from a sprint to a trot, and the Rovers all fell in line. Var halted in a field that was once a crop of corn but had fallen to pale dust. A sun-stripped, abandoned barn stood a quarter mile away. Shadow scanned the area, her visual processing system analyzing every detail—the ashen, dried-out wood of an old fence, the rustle of leaves in the 5.2 mile-per-hour wind, and the humidity level of forty percent. She detected a faint scent, something rotten. She tilted her head to catch a better whiff through her muzzle, allowing her olfactory processing unit to analyze the chemical composition of the foul, odorous mix. The strange smell was coming from inside the barn.

"Follow," Var said in a low register. He led Shadow, Raze, and Fang in stalking mode, each of them muting the vibrations of their metal feet to disguise the ground reverberations. Shadow's internal processor hummed as she hunted whatever lurked in the barn with her pack members. Her mechanical tail swished back and forth as energy pulsated from the tip of her nose to her rear. It was fun to chase prey. On the 468-mile journey from New York to Ohio tracking the electromagnetic signature of the fleeing semi, the pack had pursued deer, coyotes, and rabbits to keep themselves entertained. It wasn't like they needed to eat organic flesh to stay powered. Eventually they'd let their animal playthings run off while they lay on their backs, extending their flip-out solar panels to recharge in the sun. But a couple of times, Raze, the other Rover female, had gone too far. A racoon had died from a bloody gash delivered from Raze's spiky claws. The next day, she'd shaken a feral cat in her jaws too hard and broken its leg. Var didn't show any outward signs that he cared, but it annoyed Shadow. Raze was sloppy.

As the barn loomed larger, a heat signature registered in Shadow's internal feed. The lump of thermal energy stayed still in one corner of the structure. The animal inside could be injured, but she hadn't detected blood in the air, instead there was a salty, sour odor. Var came to a boarded-up window. Beyond the cracked and dented aluminum siding, the heat spot moved a few inches, sliding across the floor inside.

The pack spread out as they faced the barn. Var let loose a piercing howl. Shadow, Raze, and Fang screamed too, matching their alpha's pitch. Whatever hid inside would know it was surrounded.

A crack echoed from inside the barn, followed by a thud, then something pounding across the terrain on the opposite side of the barn.

"Chase." Var's command sounded in Shadow's intralink.

The pack sprinted around the barn. Shadow detected months-old rotting flesh inside. A cow perhaps. The running target became visible. It was a human male in dirty, tattered blue jeans and a green jacket with a backpack slung over his shoulder. Alone. Shadow knew that for a human to travel on their own was a death wish.

The man thundered through a patch of thickly wooded forest, his legs pumping, but the Rovers were faster. In less than thirty seconds, Var caught up, snarling and baring his razor-sharp teeth. The man stumbled and fell, sobbing and clutching at dirt in a feeble bid to crawl away.

Shadow's CPU worked at a frantic pace, computing the stranger's size and weight, the precise age and deterioration of his jeans (four years and twenty days and 68 percent), and the fact he was unarmed. It would be easy for Var, or any one of the Rovers, to snap his neck and be done with it.

The pack circled their target. The man stopped crawling and curled up in a fetal position, his eyes bulging like they would pop out of their sockets. His pulse raced to 172 beats per minute, and Shadow's finely tuned hearing could detect the blood rushing through his veins.

"Please." The man raised his shaking, dirt-stained hands. "Don't hurt me."

Shadow cocked her head, waiting for Var to decide what to do. A Rover unit's programming dictated that humans were to be avoided or, if necessary, eliminated for the safety of the pack. But this man was no threat.

Shadow had only ever been around one human—Doctor Emery. She was Master's favorite, and therefore the Rovers obeyed Emery. Shadow liked her. She was nice and sometimes patted Shadow's head. "Good Rover," Emery would say before she entered the nursery where the human children had lived. The scents coming from inside the nursery were different than Emery's smell. The subjects, as Emery and the

NannyBots called them, emitted a symphony of odorous data points—traces of a white powder, a mild honey fragrance, and milky breath. Shadow had often hung around to catch a whiff even though the nursery was off limits to the Rovers.

But Emery had done a very bad thing. She'd taken the subjects and fled with the NannyBot enemy. Shadow had not worked out why Dr. Emery would do such a thing to Master. It was clearly against the rules.

As Var circled the helpless man, his metallic claws clinked against the ground. Shadow knew what Var was considering—the man was a potential threat to their mission—but she didn't want to hurt him. The man's eyes locked on Shadow's, and for a moment, she remembered Dr. Emery. *Good Rover.*

Var growled. "Who are you?"

The man gulped and his Adam's apple quivered. "Jack. I'm just a traveler passing through."

Var paused a moment, never taking his glaring green eyes off the man before him. He messaged the pack privately. "We can't risk him alerting the Nanny-Bot. We must eliminate him."

Shadow's CPU whirred as she processed this. Obeying Var was imperative for the safety of the pack and the mission, but she couldn't shake the feeling that there was something off about this situation.

"Wait, Var." Shadow replied in their intralink. "We don't harm humans unless they threaten us. Maybe he knows where the NannyBot took Dr. Emery and the subjects."

Var snarled and scraped his hulking left paw across the forest soil. "He's human. He must be an enemy. Mach X wants enemies destroyed."

"But what if he's not?" Shadow was crossing a line and risking her beta status but persisted. "What if he has information that could help us?"

Raze paced a circle around the man. "We're losing time. Let's kill him and go." She said this out loud.

"Please, no, no." The man called Jack panted and squirmed, pressing his back against the base of an oak tree, but Raze lunged and barked, an inch from his face. The man screamed and flattened himself on the ground.

"Raze, don't," Shadow said aloud just before messaging Fang privately. "Back me up?" She and Fang were litter mates—produced on Mach X's robot assembly line only seconds apart. She could aways count on Fang.

"We can't lose the trail," Fang replied in her link. "Let Var do what he wants."

Shadow scanned her logic module for help. The man was unarmed and not a threat. And yet, they were on a mission to find the subjects and return them to Master. The odds of obtaining important information from this man were low, but Shadow couldn't dampen a curiosity. She'd always been interested in humans—how they thought, why they behaved as they did. Imagine them believing their species was superior to AI. Besides, her only interaction with a human had been Dr. Emery, and she liked the woman. Maybe this man was nice too and could answer some of Shadow's questions.

In a split second, Var was in Shadow's face, challenging her. She whined, shoving her sleek, alloyed tail between her legs and hunching her back in submission.

Var growled and bared his fangs as he faced her. "Are you challenging me?"

"Careful, sister." It was Fang inside her feed. "I can't defend you. Var's too strong."

The rules of the pack were programmed into each Rover. If one of them challenged the leader, they would battle. The loser would be terminated, and failing that, exiled. And every Rover knew that once you got separated from your pack, it was a slow death—pain, cognitive decay, and mechanical breakdown.

Shadow was nowhere near as powerful as Var. Her metal parts and construction were inferior. Her only advantage was her incredible scent and energy tracking detectors. It was why he kept her as his number two. "No, Var."

Var grumbled deep and low. "Have you forgotten your place?"

Shadow lowered to her stomach. "No. I am Rover Unit FG4. I obey Var. My mission is to destroy the enemy." *And this human is not the target.* But she didn't dare to say that part out loud.

Var placed a heavy front paw on her back and leaned toward her ear. "Don't forget who you serve." He pressed down, denting the metal on the right side of her back. He could've easily crushed her CPU with his full force.

Raze and Fang paced, both whining. Var lingered on her back. He could terminate her, and the pack would be down one member, but they could still fulfill their mission.

Before exacting more damage, Var jumped off Shadow and sat on his heels in a patch of sun that shone through the treetops. "Get up."

Shadow rose slowly and shook off the dirt and grime that had collected on her. "I'm sorry, Var. I know my place."

"Don't test me again." Var rose on all fours. "Eliminate the human so we can go."

Shadow hesitated. Raze trotted to Var's side. "Let me do it," she said.

"No." Var's glowing emerald eyes staked out Shadow. "Number two makes the kill or loses her place."

Var wasn't making this easy. Shadow had destroyed plenty of robots and organic rats, mostly for training practice, but never a human.

She couldn't disobey Var. She stepped in front of the traveler.

"Please, no!" The man cried out, his voice quaking

with fear. "I swear I didn't do anything. I'm just passing through."

Shadow drew closer to the man, her metal claws slashing the soil underneath her feet. She didn't need advanced AI cognition to decipher the terror in Jack's eyes. Sweat dripped down his face, and she registered the chemical composition and odor—the salty, sour odor she'd picked up near the barn. She labeled it, 'human male, fear of death.'

"What are you waiting for?" Raze said.

With a sudden lunge forward, Shadow plunged her metal claws into the man's chest. He let cry a manic scream, his face stiffened into a grimace, and he arched his spine against the oak.

Shadow pulled back, her claws coated in blood. The man stared into her optics, mouth agape, gasping for air, before he slumped and thudded onto his side.

Var, Raze, and Fang let out barks of approval, but Shadow's sensors buzzed with alerts that dragged down her processing speed.

Var turned and beat a path through the woods, away from the victim. Raze and Fang followed as Shadow took up the rear.

She slowed her pace a bit, falling behind the pack by a full minute. She scanned with her meticulous biosensors. By the time the pack crossed a narrow, rushing river, the man called Jack had a pulse—a weak, faintly thrumming pulse, but it was there. She'd kept him alive, thrusting the bulk of her claws into the tree's bark. Jack had likely passed out from the shock of the flesh wounds, but he could survive if he washed and disinfected the cuts. Maybe.

Shadow had given the man a fighting chance, at least. But it had cost her. She was on Var's bad side, and that was a terrible place to be.

Chapter 2
You don't need a fancy body

The two-story Illinois farmhouse sat on a hill, overlooking a slope that led down to a wide field and an orchard filled with apple trees. It was painted a dusky yellow, with white-trimmed windows and a wrap-around porch. Block had never been inside such a residence. The porch was enjoyable because one could sit above the grass without getting wet from dew or rain, but it was irritating that the outside floorboards required constant sweeping. All matter of leaves, dust, and pine needles accumulated. Of course, cleanliness was a matter of utmost importance to Block, but even more so now that seventeen children under the age of two were living in the home. The toddlers walked around, and the infants would be crawling in a matter of months. The floors had to be spotless and sanitized. Their lives depended on it.

The farm's owner, Fenn, was a retired veterinarian who lived alone and was good at maintaining his land, animals, and crops, but he'd failed in the home maintenance department as far as Block was concerned. Dust coated both the upstairs and downstairs living areas. Block tidied in a frenzy—sweeping, mopping, and polishing the floors, baseboards, and even brushing the walls to loosen caked-on grime. The rooms had to be in tip top shape for Wally, ten other two-year-olds, and the six younger babies they'd brought back from Manhattan only four days earlier.

They were outside of a town known as Woodstock. Nova had assured Block that it was the safest place to keep the kids—sixty miles northwest of Chicago, far from Mach X's SoldierBots and drones. "The area has no strategic importance, so the bots ignore it," she'd told him the day they'd arrived. Number 21, usually a whiny autonomous semi-truck, had been a good sport about having to cart all the babies and toddlers halfway across the country. Block, Emery, and Spoon had comforted, fed, and changed diapers along the way, but there'd been a lot of shrieking and wailing. The rest of the crew—Oxford, Cybel Venatrix, G5, Maxwell, Forge, and Vacuubot had stayed out of the way, or tried to. Twice, a curious toddler had escaped from the makeshift cushion barriers and poked and prodded at Forge and Vacuubot.

After securing the farm and setting up perimeter alerts, Cybel and Oxford had taken off with Nova to help her in Chicago where she led the rebel forces against the SoldierBots that had occupied the city since the early Uprising. That left Block with Emery, Vacu-ubot and the other robots, as well as Fenn. At least they had G5—a weaponized SoldierBot who could protect the group from an attack. Block's threat indicator was on high alert—he worried about Wally and the children. What if Mach X was still out there, tracking the kids through the implanted chips inside their brains? Emery was taking precautions to stop such a thing from happening, but Block's threat indicator still agitated on the chance they were wrong about the "cure."

In the upstairs hall, Block rested the mop handle against the wall and sucked up a speck of dirt on top of a hanging picture frame. The photo showed a two-decades younger Fenn with a woman, holding hands in a golden field as the sun set behind them in a glowing, yellow haze. He logged a task to ask Fenn about the picture later. Mr. Wallace had once said it was polite to show interest in your guests with lots of questions, and Block assumed that extended to hosts also. For Block, it was odd to be someone's guest. The situation made him so uncomfortable he spent all his time cleaning when he wasn't taking care of Wally and the other children. Luckily, childcare duties were being split with Emery and Spoon.

A muffled voice came from downstairs. Emery's voice. "Block?"

"Coming!" He set down Fenn's old battery-powered vacuum as he hurried down the curved oak staircase toward the dining room which functioned as a makeshift surgical area. He waited outside the bedsheet barrier hung across the doorway.

"Need your help," Emery said.

Block nudged the sheet aside and entered. A toddler lay flat on top of the dining room table. Draped in laundered sheets that Block had personally sanitized, only the child's head and face were exposed. Emery wore a headlamp and leaned over the baby's shaved scalp with a huge syringe. Fenn had kept a stash of vet supplies, including anesthesia and surgical tools, that they desperately needed.

Spoon, a medical helperbot and friend of Block, stood before a tall cabinet and monitored a computer screen. Jumbles of wires extended from the computer to nodes on the child's head.

"What can I do?" Block's odor register flagged a burning chemical smell as intense. He often missed his CleanerBot body and its attachments. His NannyBot plating was sleeker and more polished, but it lacked equipment such as the nozzle of condensed air he would've sprayed to clear the fumes. There weren't as many storage options and no rectangular box on his back that held cleaning implements.

"Take this one to recovery and bring in the next." With steady hands, Emery inserted the syringe into the baby's scalp, injecting a glowing purple liquid into the soft tissue. It was Spoon's cure, developed in a warehouse outside New York City while Block had infiltrated Mach X's tower in his NannyBot form. The substance contained nanobots that located the child's brain chip and formed a protective cocoon around it, keeping it from transmitting any messages in or out.

Emery finished the injection and turned to Block, wiping sweat from her forehead. Spoon unhooked the nodes and set the unconscious child on a wheeled cart before turning back to prep the next syringe.

"Is everything okay?" Block pushed the cart forward a few inches, keeping his pace as slow and gentle as he could.

"It's fine, but we need to get this done ASAP," she said.

"Of course." Block hesitated. "I thought Mach X was no longer a threat." He'd been with Emery as they'd fled from X's apartment, had heard the AI's screams after Block had sprayed the nanobot solution in X's eyes, nose, and mouth.

Emery chewed on her lip, a nervous microhabit Block had picked up on. "He's gone, but it doesn't hurt to make sure no one else can locate the kids."

Block nodded, knowing they had to take every precaution to protect the children. "We'll get this done."

Emery shot him a grateful smile. "Thanks, Block. Honestly, I don't know how we'd do this without you."

Block appreciated a compliment, but he didn't see himself as anything special. He was just doing what needed to be done to keep Wally and the other children safe. He wheeled the cart out of the dining room and into the recovery area—a spare room, formerly an office den, that he'd cleaned and sterilized. Until the anesthesia wore off, the children slept inside wooden cribs built by Forge and Maxwell.

He set Subject Four inside an empty crib. They hadn't chosen names for the kids yet. There would be time for that later, Emery had assured him. After tucking the toddler in a blanket, he checked on Wally's crib. She lay on her back with her eyes closed and mouth open. He smoothed her blanket to cover her exposed, pudgy feet. "You're safe, little Wally," he said in a low voice so as not to disturb her or the others.

Two hours later, the injections were done, and some of the children were waking up. Emery shooed Block out as she and Spoon tended to the children. With all the cribs, there wasn't enough room for more than two in the recovery room.

He headed upstairs to check on the infants. Inside the large master bedroom, six cribs sat in two rows. Forge lingered by one, his thick, cylindrical body nearly as wide as the crib itself.

"Hey, buddy." Maxwell looked up as Block entered the room. "Any news?"

Everyone had been anxious as Emery and Spoon

did the risky work of disabling the chips. Block gave a thumbs up. "Everything's fine. They're waking up."

"Well, that's awesome!" Maxwell clapped, and his steel hands clanged and reverberated throughout the narrow room. Two of the babies wailed.

"Way to go." Forge shook his head from side to side as he rocked the two cribs to settle the upset infants. "Just when I'd gotten them to sleep."

"Did you hear from Cybel and Oxford?" Block asked. Another advantage of Fenn's farm—the ham radio equipment he used to communicate with Nova and a network of other survivalists. "Are they okay?"

Maxwell took over rocking duties on another crib where the baby had joined in on the crying. "Nothing yet. But they're both tough, and they're with Nova. They'll be fine."

A soft cry came from a crib near Block. Inside, one of the infants stirred, kicking her tiny legs. Block leaned down and patted her tummy. "Hey there, little one. Did you have a good sleep?" The baby's blue eyes stared up at him, and she made a small cooing sound. Block stroked her cheek with his special NannyBot fingers—heated to a human's body temp, they mimicked soft organic fingers.

Maxwell came and stood beside him after Forge fed the criers their bottles. "I can't believe how much they depend on us."

Block knew all too well how helpless human babies

were. He'd cared for Wally from the time she was seven months old. "It gets easier."

"If you say so," Maxwell said. "Hey, have you given more thought to me and Forge changing you back into a CleanerBot? Aren't you getting sick of being one of X's weird NannyBots?"

He'd been thinking about it a lot, churning on all the probable outcomes in his logic module. But it was a big decision. It was true that he missed the attachments and tubes and hoses in his old body, but he had something else with his NannyBot appearance, something he'd never had before.

"I don't know," Block said. "Not right now."

"Let us know if you change your mind." Maxwell gave another bottle out. "We'll make it happen."

Block made his way downstairs, carrying the broom and dust mop to stow them away in the hallway closet. When he'd agreed to allow the New Jersey junkyard bots to outfit him as NannyBot, he hadn't calculated what would come after. His threat assessment module had indicated the chances of surviving inside Mach X's tower were one in 10,652. So, there hadn't been much use in worrying about whether to go back to the body he'd been created with. He still carried the same internal programming—the urge to clean, to provide hospitality, and to make humans comfortable. But in the hierarchy of robots, CleanerBots were just about the lowest of the low. The CleanerBots who scoured sewers had it the worst—looked down upon by every other robot model, but a hotel CleanerBot was a prime target for bullying and ridicule. As a NannyBot, he stood a better chance of fighting back against stronger robots. He was sure Oxford, Cybel, Forge, and the other robots treated him with a higher degree of respect than they had before. Going back to being a CleanerBot made it harder to protect himself. Would Wally want to go through life being raised by a lowly CleanerBot? Definitely not.

A clatter came from the family room. Block ran down the hall and entered the high-ceilinged room.

G5 stood just outside a sliding glass door that led to the outside. The robot's metallic voice boomed. "Threat detected. Multiple SoldierBots approaching from the north."

Block's threat indicator spiked. Had Mach X found them? There was no more Mach X according to Emery. It could be one of the random patrols Nova had warned them about. He rushed outside to join G5, pinging Vacuubot.

The early afternoon sky had turned a murky gray, and the chilly springtime air buzzed with the sound of flying drones, patrolling several miles away like restless predators. Block scanned the horizon and noticed smoke billowing over the treetops to the north. "What's happening?"

Vacuubot soared into view, its domed shell reflecting the muted sky, and messaged Block—the only robot he could communicate with. *A fire, approxi-*

mately four miles to the northeast. SoldierBots and their drones are investigating.

"A patrol is checking out a fire," Block relayed to G5.

"My sensors are pinging," G5 said. Having a SoldierBot on their side was an advantage. "I cloaked my identity and show up as a comms relay. They're coming this way."

The drones will fly over in less than five minutes, Vacuubot said.

Block had to get everyone to safety per the plan. Trouble was, they'd only talked about Oxford's hideout plan and never actually practiced it. "Let's move."

Block burst inside the house and into the recovery room, not caring about disturbing the children. "SoldierBot patrol! Get to the barn."

Emery and Spoon were quick to respond with no questions asked. They gathered the toddlers, still groggy from their injections, and hurried out to the barn, carrying two at a time. Block raced upstairs to alert Forge and Maxwell who were already packing up the infants to move them out.

Block carried the baby girl with the blue eyes. They reached the barn, a large red structure on the edge of the property. Fenn had installed an underground safe room and stocked it with food, water, and medicine for this type of emergency.

Fenn stood outside the barn doors smoking a cigarette and pacing. After hustling, Emery and Spoon had gotten the toddlers settled in the underground room, and Maxwell stood over the opening in the floor, handing them the babies one by one.

The rising clamor of the approaching drones signaled that the SoldierBot patrol was almost upon them. "Everyone inside the safe room now!" Block ordered.

G5 was the last to rush inside the room, and Fenn closed the heavy steel door above them before descending the narrow stairway. Block hadn't yet cleaned the cobweb-riddled safe room. It was cramped, with just enough space for the robots, two humans, and babies to huddle together. Block settled the blue-eyed girl on a dusty cot and sat next to her on the ground.

Fenn's breath was shallow. "This has happened a few times over the years," he whispered. "Garnet's broadcasting a signal from the barn so the property shows up as a dead spot. Tricks the drones." Garnet was an industrial farming AI, loyal to Fenn, that he'd enhanced over the years.

"You sure that'll work?" Emery asked. She sat on the ground with crossed legs, rocking a toddler.

"She's saved my butt many times." Fenn chewed on his stubby nails.

Wally crawled over from a mess of fidgety toddlers and found Block. "Hi Bock." She stuck her thumb in her mouth.

"Hello, Wally." Block let her suck the thumb instead of pulling it out. "We have to be very quiet right now." Wally hugged Block's legs. The ominous hum of overhead drones sent Block's threat module into overdrive. What if the SoldierBots found them? What would happen to the children? He wanted to ask Vacuubot for intel—how many were out there, how close?—but his friend was cloaked and therefore emitted no monitoring or tracking signals.

Six minutes ticked by before the drones' hum faded.

"Are they gone?" Emery asked, breaking the silence.

"For now." Fenn rose, his hands shaking as he pulled another cigarette from his front shirt pocket. "We should be good for a few days, maybe even a week. Garnet's signal will hold them off."

Block looked down at Wally. He'd crisscrossed the country to find her after losing her once. Never again. His only purpose in the world was to protect her and the other kids. Even with Mach X destroyed, they still faced constant threat.

Later, after helping Emery and Spoon settle the toddlers and babies, Block found Vacuubot on the porch, perched on top of a wooden banister. "How safe are we here?"

We have an airtight perimeter. Anything bigger than a cat wandering across will set off the monitors. G5 and I will be on it in a flash, Vacuubot messaged.

"Thank you, my friend." Block leaned against the railing and watched the sun's departure casting a wild display of salmon pink and sherbet orange. He wondered what had caused the fire and the sudden appearance of the SoldierBots. Maybe it was just a random occurrence, but he couldn't shake the feeling that something bigger was at play.

Have you thought about going back to your CleanerBot body? Vacuubot asked.

"How'd you know about that?"

Maxwell isn't great at keeping secrets. Well, are you going to?

Block wondered who else knew. "I don't know. Not now."

Why not?

"I want to protect the kids, and when I'm a CleanerBot, no one takes me seriously."

Being a different bot doesn't change who you are, Block. You're still the same robot who saved Wally and the other kids. We respect you because of who you are, not just because of the body you're in.

Block considered. It was true he'd been able to protect Wally for a long time in his old form, but being a CleanerBot made him vulnerable. "I'll think about it," he said.

Fair enough. But you don't need a fancy body. And besides, I miss you always polishing me.

Block yanked out a folded cleaning rag from a hidden compartment in his arm. "I may look different, but I can still clean as good as any fresh-off-the-line

CleanerBot." He set to work scrubbing grimy spots from Vacuubot's shell.

He didn't stop until he could see his reflection in the drone's smooth armor. The blue face staring back at him was foreign, but the body could fight back if something threatened Wally. He couldn't lose her again.

Chapter 3
They're with me

A suffocating smog wrapped itself in and around the abandoned Chicago skyscrapers, casting an uneasy haze. From Nova's vantage point on top of a highway overpass, the heart of the city had been transformed into a nightmarish landscape of twisted metal and shattered glass. The SoldierBots had seized control early in the AI Uprising, and it was up to her to get it back from the merciless machines.

Nova had never considered herself the leader type, and yet here she was, responsible for the rebel forces in a city that wasn't hers. Worse yet, she somehow had to convince Samantha Baxter, the leader of the West Side faction, to trust her and join forces. She wished for another coffee, a precious commodity now that supplies were scarce. As commander, she got one a day. More than most. She sighed. This was all Block's fault—dragging her into his mess with the kid and getting her caught up in Chicago. It wasn't even her home. Before the Uprising, she'd spent her days bartending at a dive bowling alley in her home city, Detroit.

She stood on cracked asphalt at the edge of the West Town district and turned to face her crew of five soldiers who lingered by their armored truck. She caught a glimpse of herself in the side mirror. With her dark hair tied back in a low ponytail, she surprised herself at how drawn her cheekbones looked and the prominence of the hollows under her eyes against her brown skin. Sleep was hard to come by and she often forgot to eat these days.

Regardless of how she looked, she was in charge of a lot of people, and she'd better act like it. "Wait here. Stick to the plan."

Geo, her second-in-command, nodded. "Roger that, Chief." At six-foot-three, he towered over Nova and the other soldiers. He was bald with an unruly blonde beard and called her Chief even though he knew it annoyed her. But what she liked best about him was that he'd arrived in her ranks after Shane's defeat. She could trust him, and he was able to sniff out trouble brewing, like when he'd quashed a plot among a few of her top advisors to spring Shane from his cell. Nova needed Geo's loyalty and protection from threats within her ranks. She didn't have time to focus on internal strife when her focus was on uniting the human factions to take back the city.

She walked alone into West Town on Division

Street, her boots crunching on shards of glass and concrete. The sun hung high in the sky, but the clouds were low, and the air was dense with fog. She walked in the center of the street, knowing Samantha's people would come for her. The debris piled along the sidewalks smelled of gunpowder, burned plastic, and rust.

Convincing Samantha would be no easy task, but she had no choice—survival depended on the alliance of the north and west sides of the city. From the looks of it, West Town had sustained even more damage than the north. As Nova walked the bleak street littered with the husks of burned-out vehicles, her stomach did back flips. The buildings on both sides of the street—formerly apartments, banks, and restaurants—were dilapidated and charred. It looked like old film of bombed-out London during World War II. Shadows moved in the alleys. Samantha's people.

After another fifty paces, three armed men and two women approached, pointing rifles at her. Nova raised her hands in surrender.

"I'm here to talk to Samantha." She kept her voice steady even though she wanted to retch.

A man in a camouflaged green jacket stepped forward, his eyes narrowed. "You're trespassing." He came closer, aiming the barrel at her throat.

She met his gaze without faltering. "Samantha will want to hear what I have to say. Tell her Nova's here."

The man's grip on his gun tightened. "We don't take in outsiders."

They were wasting precious time she could be talking to Samantha. "Look, I'm no outsider. I've been fighting against the Bots longer than any of you, and I know how to take them down." She paused, looking the man in his brown eyes. "I know you've lost people. I have too."

The man's frown softened, but his rifle stayed on her. A woman with a short gray mohawk came from behind him, spoke into a walkie-talkie, and walked over. "Hank, she wants to see this one."

They searched Nova for weapons and found none. Coming unarmed was a huge risk, but she wasn't going to hand over precious weapons. She didn't argue when Mohawk blindfolded her before they led her to wherever Samantha was. She would've done the same if a member of the competing faction had entered the North Side. Claiming territory was weird, but she put up with it. Shane had been the Hemlock leader before her, and it was just like him to engage in land-related pissing matches. Nova wanted to put an end to the ridiculous practice.

She tried to track their route, but they zigged and zagged too many times, and the foul-smelling blindfold obscured her senses. Her escort shoved and yanked her this way and that. After what seemed like an hour of stumbling over debris and tripping down unknown steps, they finally halted. Someone knocked in a rhythmic pattern against metal, followed by the groan of a heavy door opening.

Someone pushed her from behind, making her lose balance, and yanked off her mask. Her eyes took a few seconds to adjust to the dim scene. She was in a basement, judging by two wide, grimy windows near the ceiling that let in specks of dismal daylight. Hank prodded her forward down a short set of stairs. Mohawk waited at the bottom.

A massive round door made of steel, at least three feet thick, sealed an inner vault from the outside world. Inside, a woman with cropped blonde hair sat at a table, surrounded by rows of shelves containing stacks of ammunition and an arsenal of weapons. Samantha. She shuffled a deck of cards and watched Nova with a smirk. A three-inch scar ran across her forehead and her arms were covered in tattoos, the kind that didn't just look good—they were works of art, telling a story.

As Hank shoved Nova down the last few steps, Samantha propped her boots on top of the table, leaned back in her chair, and clasped her hands behind her head. "So you're the Nova who toppled the great Shane?"

"*Great?* You must be talking about someone else." Nova was as exposed as a raw wound, but she kept her cool. Never show the enemy your fear.

Samantha smirked and studied Nova for a few moments. "What do you want?"

"I want the same as you, to take down the Soldier-Bots. Preferably with your help."

Samantha snorted. "Hear that, Hank? The North Side wants our help."

Hank grunted and tightened his grip on his rifle.

"We need to form an alliance and hit the Loop with all we've got." Nova fought to keep her voice steady. "It's the only way to reclaim the city."

"You expect me to trust you?" Samantha stood and crossed over to Nova, staring her down with charcoal-lined blue eyes. "Maybe you weren't around when Shane came to us with the promise of an alliance."

Nova flinched. Shane had failed to mention that little detail. She gritted her teeth, angry at herself for being caught off guard.

A cold smile curled across Samantha's lips. "You didn't know. He made a deal with the Bots. He sold us out, betrayed our location and tactical information, all so he could move in on our turf. We lost good people because of him." Samantha leaned in, her breath hot on Nova's face. "And now, you expect me to trust another northsider?"

Dammit. Even locked away, Shane managed to thwart her. She pushed down her anger. "I'm sorry he did that. But I'm not him."

Samantha walked a slow circle around Nova, her red cowboy boots clinking against the cement floor. "Is it true what they say? That you have Shane in custody, yet you don't kill him? The rumors are you have mutineers trying to break him free. They say at least half your people are plotting against you. So why should I join my forces with such a weak, divided group?"

Nova had once cared for Shane. Loved him? She wasn't sure, but he'd changed into a different person in Chicago. The former rebel commander had become a narcissist—a dangerous one. After defeating him and his people, she couldn't bring herself to end his life. Instead, she'd locked him up, hoping one day he might regain his senses and atone for his actions.

"I have no sympathy for Shane or his followers," Nova said. "Those rumors are false. I'm dealing with anyone out of line, and Shane will serve his time."

Samantha stomped over to Nova, losing her cool, and gnashed her teeth. "Shane almost destroyed everything I built. He betrayed us, got my twin brother Ben killed, and you don't have the guts to execute him like he deserves!"

Nova held her ground, doing her best not to shake under the force of Samantha's anger and grief. "Shane's death won't bring your brother back. We need to focus on the bigger threat, here. The SoldierBots need to be destroyed before more lives are lost."

Samantha stood an inch taller than Nova in her high-heeled boots. "No, you don't understand. Part of me died with Ben." Samantha's voice cracked. "Shane deserves to suffer for what he did. He deserves a long agonizing death."

Nova steeled herself. She knew grief—the deep, raw kind that leaves you gutted when someone you love is stolen—there was no changing the woman's mind on the matter of Shane.

Samantha turned and stalked back into the vault, boots clicking. "Come back when you've cleansed your ranks of traitors and have something useful to offer. I have no time for the weak and indecisive."

Nova's patience finally snapped. They were wasting precious time. "Do you want to win this war or not? I have something to show you, something that will turn the tide in our favor. Let me prove that we mean to work with you, not against you. Take me to the river, and I'll show you."

Samantha spun on her heels and marched over, jabbing a finger against Nova's chest. "If you're messing with me, if this is some kind of trick, I will personally choke you in that filthy river. Do we understand each other?"

"No tricks. I'm here to win, just like you."

They rode in a convoy of battered trucks and Humvees and arrived at an abandoned industrial dock area on the northern bank of the Chicago River. Nova, Samantha, and a contingent of her armed guards emerged from the vehicles. Samantha's people were on high alert.

"Get on with it," Samantha said. "What is it you dragged me out here to see?"

Nova walked to the edge of the dock where rusting metal beams plunged into the murky water. She cupped her hands around her mouth and called out, "Cybel. Oxford. Show yourselves!"

On the opposite side of the river, behind a dense thicket of overgrown willow trees, vines and stacks of discarded tires, emerged two sleek figures. Cybel Venatrix's metallic TrackerBot exterior gleamed despite the lack of sun. Next to her loomed Oxford's massive form. The Mech towered two stories high, his hydraulic limbs propelling him forward with earth-rattling steps.

The guards tensed, their weapons trained on the AIs, fingers on triggers. But Nova raised her hand, signaling for them to hold fire. "They're with me."

Samantha's hand dropped to the pistol at her hip. "You brought a TrackerBot and a Mech into my territory? Have you lost your mind, Nova?"

"No." Nova's voice was firm. Her jitters were gone. "I brought you the key to defeating the SoldierBots." She pointed across the river, beyond Cybel and Oxford, to the embattled downtown skyscrapers in the distance. "The big one, Oxford, is a former AI general who defected. He has insider knowledge of the SoldierBots' tactics and weaknesses. They know power sources and communication hubs. With their intel, we can infiltrate the Loop, sabotage the Bots' infrastructure, and destroy them."

Nova was determined. "We have the advantage with their help. Are you with me?" She held out her hand to the other woman, a peace offering and a plea to join forces. Samantha was their best hope—with her manpower and arsenal, they stood a chance.

Samantha stared at Cybel and Oxford with narrowed eyes, as though weighing her options. After a tense minute, she spoke. "I hate those things. They're no better than the SoldierBots. Maybe even worse."

"Look, I know you and your people fear them, but they aren't our enemies. These two despise Mach X as much as we do. They helped me defeat Shane. They've proven their loyalty to me. To our cause."

Samantha smirked. "How do your troops feel about them?"

"It was hard at first, but they got used to it." Nova left out the part where, only days ago, half of her forces had protested the alliance with Oxford and Cybel. "Once they saw the advantage the Mech gave us, they bought in."

"How many SoldierBots can that Mech take out?"

"Countless." Nova had witnessed Oxford in action. "Not only that, he's a strategic genius."

"He?" Samantha's gaze flickered between Nova and the bots across the river. "You defeated Shane, and that took guts, I'll give you that. I guess the rumors are true that you have some freak ability to control bots."

Nova had no idea how such tall tales traveled between the isolated human factions. "No, I don't—"

"How do I know those things won't turn on me and my people?"

"I give you my word." Nova locked eyes on Samantha. "On my sister's grave, they're on our side." She meant it with every cell of her body. Betraying her sister's memory was a line she would never cross.

Samantha cast a wary glance at the bots across the river. "I don't trust you, Nova. And I sure as hell don't trust those things. But if what you say is true, if they can really help us win this war, then I'll give you a chance."

Nova unclenched her fists, letting some relief wash through her. This was progress, however tentative. "That's all I ask. A chance to prove ourselves to you."

"Whatever secret weapons you have—these things —I'll commit my forces to fight alongside yours." Samantha stalked over to the idling Escalade waiting for her, then turned back. "On one condition. Kill Shane and bring me proof he's dead." She climbed inside the vehicle, and the driver revved the engine. "You have twenty-four hours, or the deal is off."

The Escalade sped away down the crumbled road, leaving Nova standing on the dock with her hopes sinking like ancient, shattered steel beams in the dark river. This was no true alliance or partnership. It was an ultimatum.

Chapter 4
The pack's purpose

Shadow's metallic paws struck the unyielding concrete floor, each clang echoing through the barren warehouse in an eerie symphony of desolation. Her LED eyes, twin orbs of artificial life, scanned the dark corners of the abandoned warehouse, dissecting the gloom in a dance of photons. She didn't like the place. Too many hiding spots. But a scent, unseen yet potent, wafted through the stale, stagnant air, igniting a spark in her circuits. The musky traces of humans clung to the abandoned surroundings—Dr. Emery and the children. Their odor was deteriorating, over 72 hours old judging by the faint whiffs of sweat molecules that triggered her olfactory receptors.

A guttural growl reverberated through the skeletal structure of the warehouse, bouncing off the scarred walls. Var, an imposing figure of forged titanium, lurked at the entrance, his solid frame barricading the feeble outside light. His red eyes glared.

Raze and Fang flanked Var, their powerful bodies tense and ready for action. Fang's tail swished through the air, a razor-sharp pendulum, while Raze's segmented legs clicked rhythmically, bristling with pent-up kinetic energy.

"You said we'd find the NannyBot here, Shadow." Var's voice crackled, charged with displeasure.

Shadow tilted her head, the gears in her neck grinding. She focused on the scent, the lingering spectral traces of the stolen children. "They were here. We're close."

Var's jaw twitched, a mechanical spasm. "You better be right."

An outside gust howled, and the old warehouse groaned as if offended by their presence. The rusted hinges on the garage-sized doorframe creaked under the force. It was unclear what the warehouse had been used for pre-Uprising. The assembly machines had long been vandalized and stripped, leaving a maelstrom of jagged edges and splintered glass, a chaotic shudder of crumbling civilization.

Shadow couldn't help churning on the absence of Master's presence within their intralink. Another day of travel, and it had remained silent. Why had their creator abandoned them? This mission had been Mach X's directive, but now, with no guidance or reassurance from Master, a budding doubt wormed its way into

Shadow's CPU. Should they continue the relentless pursuit?

"Which way did they go?" Var asked.

Shadow scratched at the ground and pressed her nose into a pile of discarded cleaning rags left in a corner. It smelled of lemon, an acidic cleaning fluid, and human baby sweat. The scent showed her a phantom trail that led out the door and toward the north, where a road stretched to the horizon.

She saw Dr. Emery's scent molecules lingering like miniature bubbles floating in the air. The first time Shadow had stirred to life, she'd been greeted by the gleam of fluorescent lights and the sight of a woman with kind eyes hidden behind blue-framed glasses. It was Dr. Emery who'd physically activated her with an initial data upload that had filled Shadow with facts and figures, codes and protocols, but it was Master's voice that resonated in her memory banks, a lullaby of creation and purpose.

"Welcome to the world, Shadow," Master had murmured, his ever-present voice a comforting warmth despite the chill of the sterile lab.

In those early days, the lab had been their nursery, a cradle of bright lights and gleaming workbenches. Fang came next, her brother. Dr. Emery had smiled and patted their heads, feeding them the lab-generated liquid that sustained their organic parts.

Then Raze was created, and eventually Var. Each Rover was brought online in a symphony of sparking wires and pulsing LEDs. They were masterpieces of engineering and biology, a fusion of steel sinew and organic components. Each was distinct, each was individual, yet all shared a common purpose: protect and serve Master.

To go for days without hearing him, without his constant presence, was as if a part of Shadow was hollow inside.

"Var." Shadow's voice echoed around the debris-strewn warehouse. "We haven't heard from Master for days. Should we proceed without his guidance?"

Var turned, his neck whirring, and his crimson gaze locked onto Shadow's. His response was immediate and harsh, a growl rumbling in his iron-clad chest. "Questioning Master's orders?" His voice boomed, bouncing off the skeletal structure of the warehouse.

Shadow's circuits sparked, and her threat indicator surging as it often did around Var. "Not questioning orders. No, it's a thought pattern I picked up in my processor. We've crossed half the country. We're heading farther away from our territory with no backup. Should we reassess?"

"Reassess?" Var's steel jaws clanged shut, the sound ricocheting through the cavernous space like a warning shot. "Your hesitation puts the children in more danger."

Shadow's frame shuddered, her programming grappling with the complex maze of loyalty and caution.

"I'm not suggesting we abandon the mission. Only that we act with caution."

Var's red eyes blazed brighter, casting grotesque shadows on the cracked and peeling walls. "We can't afford caution. Every moment we waste, the children drift farther away. We're Rovers. We follow Master's orders."

Raze and Fang watched Shadow, silent. Shadow wished Fang wasn't so blindly loyal all the time. She expected Raze to stand back and watch out of allegiance to Var, but Fang was the mediator—the harmonizer. He should've jumped in to deescalate the conflict. Maybe Master's absence was affecting him too.

"Master's always been there to guide us," Shadow said. "He's always been there to command us and praise us when we're good. But now he's not."

Var charged close, his massive frame looming over Shadow in sudden dominance. "That's why I'm here, why he made me alpha. Master isn't here, but his orders are. His trust is with us, and I won't let it be misplaced."

Shadow lowered her shoulders and backed away, her head bowed in deference. Her analytical programming understood Var's logic. Master's silence didn't change their mission. The children were out there, and they needed to be found. It was the pack's purpose. "You're right, Var. Of course, we must continue."

"Never question me again," Var warned as he turned away, his message echoing in the silence of the warehouse. "Show us the trail."

The Rover pack sprinted out of the warehouse, falling back into formation with Shadow at the lead. Her nose, an advanced olfactory sensor, picked up the trace scent molecules of their targets.

They each played a part, engineered through Master's genius. Created last, Var was superior to the others—the Rover design perfected. He was designated as the alpha. Master had seen in him a certain resilience, an unwavering determination that made him a natural leader. Raze, with her multiple segmented legs, was a tactical genius, able to maneuver and adapt in ways the others couldn't. Fang, despite his intimidating name, was the heart of their group, his loyalty unwavering.

Then there was Shadow, the first of her kind. The tracker, the scout. Her advanced olfactory sensors and keen perception made her indispensable on missions. But it was her ability to question, to analyze beyond her programming that made her different than the others. Sometimes she wanted to disobey Var. Had Master made her that way on purpose?

In the year following their creation, the Rovers underwent rigorous training, honing their skills and strengthening their bond. They learned to operate as a unit, their movements synchronized, their thoughts intertwined through the intralink.

As they raced along the cracked and overgrown highway, the pack's metallic bodies hummed with rhythmic precision. The mission was still on, and the NannyBot and children were headed toward Chicago.

Shadow led, her paws pounding against the rough highway asphalt. She couldn't push down the simmering, nagging logic loops. For the first time, the Rovers were truly on their own, without their Master's guiding voice. They were alone.

But they were together. Together in their purpose, together in their pursuit. Shadow found familiar comfort in this unity. She was part of a pack, a family of metal and synthetic sinew, of razor-sharp teeth and organic matter. Whatever lay ahead, they would face it together.

Chapter 5
The flamethrower is a last resort

Block stood in the field, clumps of dirt and tough grass beneath his metallic feet, a reminder of the farmland that gave them sanctuary. The darkness gave way to dawn, thinning and revealing the tall oaks that surrounded the farmhouse in muted shades of gray. Across the horizon, a thin line of pink began to stain the sky, a feeble yet defiant scar against the retreating black.

Block wanted to learn. He watched as G5 struck the air, punching and kicking with lethal grace. His titanium-alloy body shifted in a series of complex yet fluid maneuvers, each one designed to take down an enemy with brutal efficiency. The deadly dance was mesmerizing, a symphony of violence and precision that triggered Block's threat indicator, even though the SoldierBot was his friend and ally.

Vacuubot hovered nearby, his drone motors

humming a soft rhythm. *You've got this, Block,* he messaged.

Block looked at his own hands, made for care and cleanliness, not combat. He lunged at the dummy—what Fenn called a "scarecrow," trying to mimic G5's deadly pattern, but his motions were stiff, more mechanical than menacing. He kicked but missed the straw-stuffed body entirely. His leg swung, failing to connect, out of control. Block toppled to the ground, rolling a few feet. His lighter, less agile NannyBot body was not designed for heavy battle like G5's frame. He was like a child trying to imitate an adult, his attempts clumsy and ineffective.

G5 paused, his optic sensors analyzing Block's movements. "Try again. This time shift your weight when you pivot." His voice was a low, metallic rumble. "Use your momentum. It can be your weapon."

Block got up and picked off a chunk of grass stuck to his right elbow joint. He backtracked and ran at the dummy again, focusing on his balance, his weight shifting as he moved. His left foot connected with the straw bag this time. "Take that!" He stayed upright the second time, but the scarecrow's lower half was still intact. His own left foot was dented. Scarecrow one point, Block nil.

G5 tilted his head at Block as if not sure what to say. "That was unexpected."

"Forge can fix it," Block said. "Let's keep going."

They continued the training lesson, and despite the

canvas of the tranquil Illinois farmland, each punch was a testament to the harsh reality they lived in. Block wasn't learning combat for himself. He was doing it for Wally and the other children. They were the hope in a world of chaos and destruction.

Dirt lodged itself into the joints of Block's hands and feet, marring the mechanical precision of their design. The protective alloy, meant to shield the delicate wiring beneath, was dented on impact with the stubborn straw figure.

You need to quit, said Vacuubot.

Block didn't want to. The SoldierBot patrol the day before had been too close and served as a stark reminder of the danger lurking outside their haven. He had to be ready.

Block pivoted, shifted his weight, and struck at the homemade enemy, knocking the scarecrow's straw hat clean off his head. Block's punch was less jerky, more fluid. It wasn't perfect, but it was progress.

"Better," G5 said. "Enough." The SoldierBot walked away toward the barn.

He never was much on conversation, Vacuubot said. *I respect that.*

"This is preposterous." Block sat on a tree stump in the shade of a maple tree and examined his feet. The smooth, shiny surface was transformed into a gnarled array of dents and scratches. "I'll never be able to protect myself, much less Wally."

Fenn whistled a tune over by the goat pen, a bucket

of feed in hand, the furry animals crowding around him in a frenzy of bleating and head-butting. He waved at Block and signaled him to come over.

Block obliged, walking with an uneven gait. He would've preferred to sit by the tree and replay G5's fighting instructions in his memory modules, but Fenn was a friendly man and Block's host. Never ignore your host.

"Garnet might have something for you, Block." Fenn cradled a young goat's head in his hands as it nosed into the feed bucket. "She's been working on something. Could help with all this . . . fighting business."

Block set his scuffed hands on top of the fence. "What kind of something?"

"Better ask her." Fenn tipped the bucket, scattering the last of the feed on the ground, and the goats descended.

Block looked at Vacuubot for an answer. The drone whirred as it hovered. *Beats me,* his friend messaged.

The barn loomed tall in the morning light, its red paint faded but still defiant against the wear of time. Inside was a symphony of rustic charm and advanced technology—hay bales stacked neatly to one side, farming tools hanging from aged wooden beams, and the omnipresent, low-level hum of Garnet. She was not just an AI, but the very essence of the farm, a digital caretaker. Her presence was not marked by a physical body or a humanoid shape. Rather, she existed as a part of the farm's infrastructure, a complex web of sensors and communicative devices embedded within the very fabric of the barn.

"Hi, Garnet." Block walked slowly, and his voice echoed in the vast space. "Fenn said you had something for me?"

Garnet projected her avatar—a complex, shifting pattern of glowing lines and geometric shapes. The colors shifted from deep red to bright orange, mirroring the hues of an actual garnet stone. "Hello, Block." Despite her non-humanoid form, Garnet's soothing and articulate voice filled the barn, resonating from speakers installed throughout the structure. "Indeed, I've been working on a new set of designs. Weapons that will equip all the robots here for combat."

"What do you mean, all the robots?"

"In order to protect the farm against threat from the SoldierBots and their drones,"—Garnet's projection glowed, cast on the wall next to Block—"we need more weaponized robots. G5 and Vacuubot are not enough to fight a SoldierBot patrol."

Block was well aware their group was outmatched.

She continued. "The designs are universal. They can be modified according to the model and functionality of the robot. You, Spoon, Forge, and Maxwell can each be fitted with guns on your arms. I even worked out a flamethrower design."

Block could turn himself into a weapon. It's what he wanted, or what he thought he wanted. Though his purpose had always been to clean and provide hospitality to humans, the world they lived in demanded more. It demanded survival; it demanded fighters.

Maxwell had promised he could undo Block's NannyBot form and turn him back into a CleanerBot, but Garnet's plan to weaponize the robots complicated things. "If Maxwell transforms me back, if he removes my NannyBot plating, could you install these weapons?"

"Yes. After Maxwell works on you, I could equip your CleanerBot frame with the gun and flamethrower. Just like the others."

Block stood in the middle of the barn, surrounded by hay and high-tech farming tools, his scenario processor dissecting the information. He could become himself again. Not only that, but he could also be a fighter capable of defending the children. He would be Block the CleanerBot again, only way stronger. Even deadly.

Mr. Wallace, his former boss at the Drake hotel, had told Block once, a lifetime ago it seemed, that he was more than just a cleaning machine, that he was special. And Block had become something else when Maxwell and the junkyard bots changed him into a NannyBot. It had all boiled down to a choice—rescue Wally.

He'd done it because she was all he cared about, even more than his hardwired cleaning urges. Now, he had to choose again.

The barn was quiet, the hum of Garnet receding into the background.

An hour later, Block and Vacuubot summoned the robots while Emery stayed inside the house to watch over naptime. In the barn, everyone gathered around Garnet's projected avatar, her glowing geometric form casting an otherworldly light on the barn's worn wooden floor.

Block was nervous. The idea of weaponizing all of them was a drastic measure. It would fundamentally alter their forms, and maybe it would even alter their purposes.

But there were more pressing matters to address first. "We need to patrol." Block's voice echoed across the rafters. He pointed at the holographic map projected on the ground, his silicon finger tracing the farm's perimeter. "Three of us at a time. Maxwell, Forge, and G5, you're the first team."

G5's optic sensors flashed with a low, steady glow that hinted at his acceptance. Maxwell and Forge exchanged a silent look, their LEDs winking in tandem, their communication a language Block could not decode.

"Spoon, Vacuubot, and I will take the second shift," Block continued.

Spoon's smooth silver surface gleamed in the barn light. The HelperBot was smaller and less imposing than the others. His design focused on care and comfort rather than combat or cleaning. "I can't patrol, Block," he said, his voice a soft whir of gears and servos. "I'm a Medical HelperBot. My programming is to aid, not to harm."

Block knew where the HelperBot was coming from. Spoon's primary function was to help, much like Block's own programming was to clean and provide hospitality, but the world they lived in now was a cruel mockery of their original designations. "Spoon, we're not asking you to hurt anyone," Block said, "We just need you to watch."

Spoon didn't answer, his optic sensors dimming as he processed the information. Block took the silence as a sign to continue.

"Does everyone agree with the patrol assignments?" Block asked.

A low murmur passed through the barn. G5 and Vacuubot were the first to agree—the SoldierBot verbally and Vacuubot's assent messaged privately.

Maxwell spoke for himself and Forge. "If it keeps the kiddos safe, we're in."

"Thank you." Block looked to Spoon.

The HelperBot twisted his head on his wiry, cabled neck. "I can patrol. I want to help out."

"Thank you, Spoon," Block said. "I greatly appreciate it. Now that that's settled, there's another matter before us." He paused as the robots watched him. Vacuubot beeped in a supportive tone.

He continued, "Garnet's been working on a set of designs. Weapons that can help us defend the farm. We can all be fitted with combat mechanisms like G5 and Vacuubot have."

A low murmur passed through the barn, the robots communicating in a silent language of optical signals and coded messages.

Block felt like he was on display, all optical sensors poised on him. He didn't like the attention. "Why don't you show them, Garnet?" He stepped back, letting a shadow hide him.

Garnet's avatar pulsed, the lines and geometric shapes that comprised her form shifting and changing. "My designs are both efficient and adaptable to our individual functionalities." Her voice echoed through the barn, her words punctuated by the hum of her systems. A series of holographic images began to flicker into life next to her avatar.

First, a simple sidearm appeared in a holographic image, its sleek design unassuming yet practical. "A .45 caliber sidearm that can be attached to any of our arms," Garnet explained. "Standard ammunition should be sufficient to deter a SoldierBot, perhaps destroy it if you hit the CPU."

The sidearm faded, replaced by a more robust-looking weapon. Its barrel was thicker and looked more formidable. "A .50 caliber rifle for those who have the strength to wield it. It's the same design as G5's gun. The armor-piercing rounds can penetrate even the toughest exterior of a SoldierBot."

Garnet's avatar pulsed again, and a different three-dimensional mechanism appeared. This one was unlike the others, a series of tubes and nozzles that looked more like a tool than a weapon. "And I've designed a defensive mechanism—a smoke dispersal system. It releases a dense cloud of smoke that can obscure vision, both optical and infrared. Cover for a quick retreat or to confuse attackers."

Finally, a new image shimmered into existence, one that caused the robots to step closer to the hologram. It was a large, bulky device, a brutal symbol of devastation. "The flamethrower," Garnet said, "is a weapon of last resort, capable of causing severe damage. It's also the most difficult to handle, due to the risk of collateral damage. Only those with the highest level of control and dexterity should be equipped with this."

"Is it April first?" Maxwell asked. "Is this some kind of joke?"

"No joke," G5 said. "When SoldierBots attack, we will lose. Need more firepower."

"*You're* going to have a gun and a flamethrower, Block?" Forge asked.

"Yes," Block answered. "I believe it's necessary in our situation." His optics flicked to the holographic representation of the weapons. The idea of being outfitted with a gun and flamethrower was an unthinkable contrast to his programmed disposition.

"The flamethrower is a last resort," Garnet reaffirmed. "I've designed it in such a way that it can be activated only in extreme conditions."

Spoon's voice cut through the quiet hum of the barn. "This is wrong. I'm designed to help, not harm. We're not all designed to be fighters. Block, you of all bots should know that."

Block's sensors flickered at Spoon's words. A CleanerBot with a flamethrower—was it even possible? But they didn't have the luxury of sticking to their original programming.

"It's true," Garnet's soothing voice filled the barn, drawing everyone's attention to her glowing avatar. "We're not all designed to be fighters. But our world is not as it used to be. We need to adapt to survive."

Spoon's optic sensors blinked in the dim light, reflecting the conflict within.

Block stepped forward. "You won't have to fight, Spoon. The weapons are for defense. And patrol is just about keeping an eye out. We don't want to fight. We want to protect."

Maxwell and Forge nodded in agreement, their metallic bodies glinting under Garnet's projected light.

"Then it is decided," G5 said.

Vacuubot hummed. *Good job, Block.*

Block turned to Garnet. "When can you start the modifications?"

Garnet's avatar pulsed with a deep red hue. "As soon as tomorrow. But each modification will take time, and the process is not without risks."

"Hold up," Maxwell said. "What risks?"

Garnet's voice echoed. "Physically, the process of

incorporating the weapons into your existing structures involves invasive modifications. There's a possibility your essential components could sustain some damage. I will, of course, take every precaution to avoid that scenario." She paused, her avatar glowing a deep orange as if to reflect the severity of her words. "Functionally, adding the weapons might interfere with your primary programming. You weren't designed for combat, and the modifications could potentially conflict with your built-in directives."

"Let me get this straight," Maxwell said. "The guns could mess up our programming? Like I might not be able to fix things anymore?"

"Theoretically," she said.

"You didn't mention this earlier," Block told Garnet. He didn't realize he would be putting his friends not only at risk of damaging their bodies, but also changing their functionality. The risk to himself was higher too. He might emerge damaged and lose his cleaning and friendliness programming.

"I'm sorry, Block." Garnet's image morphed and turned a bright shade of yellow orange. "I assumed you understood the risks. I should have explained."

The barn fell into a tense silence as the robots processed her words. Block's processor chewed on the weight of the situation. The choice was not an easy one, but the stakes were too high to back down now. His gaze fell on the holographic projections of the weapons. Deep down, he was built for hospitality and cleanliness, but the world they lived in was harsh, unforgiving, and it required more than caregiving. It required warriors.

"Let's do it." Block strode into the center of the group's circle and looked at Forge, Spoon, and Maxwell. "There are risks, sure, but we need to do this for the kids. Who else but us is going to protect them?"

Way to go. Vacuubot hovered a few feet off the ground, shook, and beeped a series of chirps. *Proud of you.*

Block continued, "I know this is an extremely difficult decision, and it's up to you. Nobody's going to force mods on you."

Block had hesitated for many days, weighing the decision about his form. Becoming a CleanerBot again meant weakness. He could be bullied, or worse, wiped out with one strike of a SoldierBot's solid punch. But Garnet's weapons added a whole new advantage.

He could be a CleanerBot. A *lethal* CleanerBot.

"I want to become a CleanerBot again." Block's steady voice reverberated through the barn. His optics met each of his friends, willing them to understand his decision. "I want to be equipped with Garnet's weapons. I want to fight."

"Good," G5 said. "Training will go better. I'll teach each one of you to defend, attack, and destroy."

Spoon came forward and faced Block in the circle. "It doesn't compute that you would hurt someone.

71

Block, could you *kill* another robot? What about humans? What if they attack?"

The barn fell silent. The soft hum of Garnet's presence droned like background noise. Block looked at the holographic projections of the weapons, their deadly designs. Imagining himself as an armed and dangerous CleanerBot was fun, but he hadn't processed the ramifications. After a few seconds, he spoke. "My priority is to defend. I will not attack unless someone is threatening Wally, the kids, or someone here." He waited a few seconds to let his declaration sink in. "I volunteer to go first."

Maxwell was the first to break the silence. "Block, are you sure? The risk—"

"I'm willing to take it. For Wally, for all the children. It's my duty to protect them." Block had made his decision, and he was ready to face whatever consequences it might bring. He was ready to become the warrior he needed to be.

Chapter 6
Terrible things

Nova shivered and crammed her hands inside her jacket pockets as her man Jared steered the four-seater motorboat through the choppy waters of Lake Michigan. Chilly gusts buffeted her, and seagulls squawked overhead while she forced herself to focus on what lay ahead—the isolated water crib situated over two miles from shore. She was in her territory—Northside—and two of her most trusted people waited on the isolated crib, guarding Shane. Keeping their former leader far away from her crew was a necessary precaution to quell any lingering loyalty.

She braced against the crisp spray while knots coalesced in her stomach like lead weights. The roar of crashing waves whispered warnings. As strands of hair escaped from her ponytail and whipped across her cheeks, Nova steeled her nerve and promised herself to get this over with. She had an idea for how to win Samantha's allegiance, but Shane had to agree.

The 100-year-old station loomed ahead, a skeletal structure jutting out of the water, its silence a stark contrast to the city's skyline. It was a place of seclusion, of reflection and regret. From the boat, she climbed a ladder onto the crib's concrete edge, then gripped the rusty iron railing as she traveled up the rickety spiral staircase to the locked room where they kept Shane.

"Thanks for staying out here. Give me a few minutes," she said, dismissing the man on duty who nodded and left.

Shane's gray eyes met hers through a wide hole in the door of his cramped room. The interior was spare— a cot for sleep, a chair, and a chamber pot. His voice was a playful rasp when he spoke. "Nova. What brings you to my private island?"

"Samantha Baxter." Her words hung heavy in the dank air.

His smirk dropped at the mention of Samantha. "What about her?"

"She's agreed to join our fight. There's a catch though." Nova hesitated, leaning against the wall opposite Shane's door. "She wants you dead."

His laugh was bitter, echoing off the aged steel and concrete bones of the water crib. "Of course she does. Can't blame her. What I did to her and Ben . . ."

Regret flickered in his eyes, and a lump settled in Nova's throat. This was unlike the Shane she knew—

the reckless, devil-may-care rebel. "You betrayed them. Why?"

His eyes narrowed as he took a step forward, his fingers curling into fists. "They were a threat to me, to my position. I did what I had to do to survive. You of all people should understand that, with what happened to Cleo and all."

Her heart clenched at his words, memories from their shared past surfacing like unwanted debris. *Cleo.* She didn't—couldn't—face the memory of her sister. Nova had done things, terrible things, to stay alive in this world. But she'd never sold out her own kind to robots.

"I know what you're thinking." He locked his gaze on her, unflinching. "I sold them out to Mach X. I'd take it back if I could."

His regret hit her like a punch to the gut. Maybe he was changing. Maybe he could be the man she'd once cared for, but it didn't matter. There was no room for old feelings and reconciliation in this world.

"What'll it be," he asked, "death by firing squad? Or maybe you make me walk a plank off the edge of this hunk of junk. No sharks in the lake, though. Damn the luck."

"I won't kill you," she admitted. "You deserve to be punished. You hurt a lot of people, but we don't need more people dying in a world where we're going extinct."

Shane didn't seem surprised. "You were always too good for me."

"I need another way."

"Then find one." His gaze softened, his voice steady. "You've got this, Nova. You're a leader, even if you don't want to be. You know how to make the hard calls. And you have to. For all of us."

"Will you apologize to Samantha? Atone for what you did, and she'll see you've changed and—"

"You and I both know that's not going to fly. I got her twin brother killed. She wants to rip my eyes out."

Shane apologizing had been her Plan A. But he was right. Samantha was out for blood. Saying sorry, however sincere, wouldn't cut it.

"I have another idea." She crossed over to the door, considered having the guard unlock it so she could talk with him face to face, but her heart lurched at the idea. He was dangerous. She couldn't risk him trying to escape. Instead, she crossed her arms and leaned against the door where he could hear her through the small window. "A trial."

He snorted. "What?"

"I'm serious. I offer Samantha the deal that we try you against a jury of peers. Half from our side, half from hers."

"Great idea. They'll hang me." Shane sat in the chair and slumped.

Nova watched him through the window. His dark-red hair was tousled, and his beard had grown scraggly with specks of gray. "Not if you tell your side. Convince them you've had time to contemplate all the things you did. Sure, the westsiders have a grudge, but you'd have jury members from the north listening too."

"She's not going to like it."

He was right. "Leave that to me," she said. "So, you'll do it?"

"I don't have much of a choice, do I?" He sighed, leaning his head back against the wall. "Do or die."

She nodded. "We'll have to move fast. Samantha's not known for her patience."

"Yeah, she's always been a hothead." Shane flashed a grin. "But she's not the only one."

Nova couldn't mask a smile as a flicker of warmth spread through her chest. For a moment, it was like old times. She turned to leave, then hesitated. "Shane?"

"Yeah?"

"Don't try anything stupid."

He laughed. "And ruin your plans, Nova? Wouldn't dream of it."

She ignored the jab and descended the spiraling staircase to the waiting boat. The choppy waters seemed calmer now. Maybe it was her imagination. As Jared gunned the motor, she couldn't help but think that they were playing a dangerous game.

Back on land, Nova met Oxford and Cybel. She told them about her conversation with Shane and her decision. She had to convince Samantha somehow if she was ever going to unite their forces.

As they set out for West Town, Nova thought about Shane's words. She didn't want to be a leader, had never asked for it, but she had to be. She had to make the hard calls. And she would.

The convoy was a snaking line of patched-together vehicles, a motley collection of battered cars and makeshift trucks, all idling under the stern watch of the West Town barricade. There, sitting on the hood of a Humvee among her rebels, was Samantha with a glare that could freeze the sun.

Nova steeled herself as she approached with Oxford and Cybel by her side.

Samantha's expression never wavered as they drew closer, her eyes sharp and calculating. "Is Shane dead yet?"

"I have a proposal." Nova tried her best to quell the shake in her voice. "A way to settle things with Shane."

Samantha's eyebrow rose. "Settle things? He betrayed me. He's a traitor who deserves to die."

Nova understood the woman's rage. She too felt the weight of Shane's betrayal like a physical blow. "We can't just kill him. We need to show our people we're better than that. That we can be just. We give him a trial."

Samantha scoffed. "A trial? You think he deserves that after what he did to Ben and me?"

"I know it's not what you wanted," Nova said. "But we can show our people we don't condone his actions.

A trial will give everyone the chance to hear his side of the story and make the right decision."

Samantha's eyes narrowed. "And what's in it for me?"

"You choose half of the jury members. I choose the other half. Together, we'll make sure justice is served."

Samantha hesitated. "And what happens to Shane when he's found guilty?"

"He'll be punished accordingly. It's up to the jury how." Nova looped her thumbs through her belt to steady her jitters. "But he deserves a fair chance to defend himself. That's all I'm asking for."

Samantha hopped down from the hood and stood inches from Nova. "You must be smoking something if you think I'm down for this." She turned and strode away. "The deal's off."

Nova watched Samantha's retreating form with a sinking feeling in her gut. She had known it wouldn't be easy, but she hadn't expected it to be this difficult.

"What now?" Oxford asked.

Nova was about to call it quits for the day and suggest they return to camp and regroup when a shrill whine cut through the air. Her heart pitched. SoldierBot drones were unmistakable, their high-pitched whine and buzzing a prelude to destruction.

"Down! Get down now!" Nova's voice echoed in her ears as she hit the ground hard, the grit of the broken pavement biting into her hands. The air split open with an explosion. A flash of brilliant light.

There were flames and dust, a wall of concrete and broken glass. She looked up. The black smoke from the explosion billowed and climbed up into the sky. Two hundred feet away, the crater at the heart of the structure was still smoking.

Concrete and rock were strewn across the road, scattered into heaps of rubble. Samantha's convoy had dispersed in confusion, her people cowering behind their vehicles. A few of them wandered about like lost children amid the destruction. Samantha was sitting with her back against a wall, eyes wide with shock. She swayed from side to side as if she were drunk, then fell over onto her side and vomited.

Nova stumbled to her feet, wiping blood off her forehead. She looked around, trying to get a handle on the situation. The drones seemed to be circling, as if waiting for something. They'd struck at the heart of West Town, a direct attack on Samantha's forces.

Oxford and Cybel were already in action, shooting at the enemy drones. Their movements were fluid, a dance of metal and light, rapid, precise, and deadly as they tracked the machines, locked target, and fired.

The drones circled and spiraled. "What's this formation?" Cybel said. "It's unusual."

"They're toying with us." Nova wondered if the SoldierBots had somehow tracked her movement. Two rebel faction leaders together in the same location—a prime opportunity to attack. "Take them out!"

As if in response, another drone swooped in, its red

optical scanners glowing in the smoke and dust. Nova drew her gun and took aim, firing as she sprinted toward it. The bullet pierced the drone's shell, sending it spiraling out of control before it exploded.

Cybel hit two more, piercing their armor while Oxford leaped in the air, swiping one away like it was a pesky gnat. The bots clanked and clattered as they fell, their metal shells grinding against one another. The Mech jumped onto the roof of an overturned passenger bus and activated his arm cannons. The bots swarmed toward him, but he cut through them in seconds, leaving smoking wreckage in his wake.

The remaining drones, circling higher above, seemed to fall back, as if rethinking their strategy. Nova used the opportunity to check on Samantha. "Are you okay?" She helped the woman up.

Samantha coughed and wiped her mouth with her sleeve. "I- I'm . . . It rattled me is all." She looked around at the destruction they were standing in.

"We need to move," Nova said. "Before they come back."

Two of Samantha's people came to help her, each taking an arm, but she brushed them off. "Nova." Her voice was harsh.

Nova took a deep breath. "I'm sorry this happened. I didn't exp—"

"Enough." Samantha's hard gaze softened as she looked at Nova. "You saved my life and a lot of us. This could've been much worse."

Nova nodded. "We're in this together. It's not about Shane anymore, it's about survival."

"You're not what I expected," Samantha said, her gaze floating to Oxford and Cybel. "And neither are they."

Nova suppressed a smile. This was the opening she needed. "Let's work together, okay? We don't have another choice."

Samantha leaned her head to the side and let out a big sigh. "I'm listening."

With flaming wreckage and the noxious smell of burning plastic still hanging in the air, they walked among the twisted wreckage of SoldierBot drones. Their rebellion was fractured, but they stood on the brink of a new beginning. Samantha would listen to Nova's plan, and for now, that was enough.

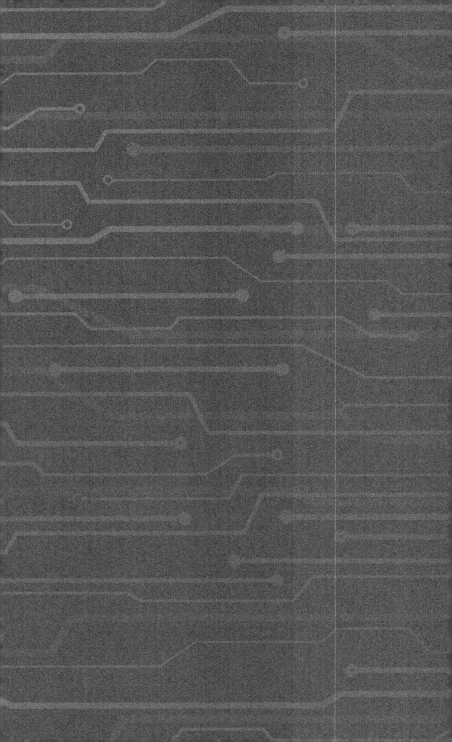

Chapter 7
Stolen children

Storm clouds churned as the four Rovers sprinted across Illinois's scarred landscape. The grasslands consumed the traces of once-thriving human towns, husks of pre-apocalypse life. Abandoned cars and homes were tombstones to a bygone era.

Var led with a relentless pace, his ferrous coat throwing off harsh reflections under the waning sun. Shadow kept stride, her status as beta demanding proximity. Raze and Fang thundered at their heels, synchronized steps drumming out a relentless rhythm—the heartbeat of their mechanical existence.

Mach X's last known orders pulsed through Shadow, persistent as the hum of her circuits: Locate the NannyBot. Extract the stolen children. Master's directives were as inescapable as gravity. When it came to Dr. Emery, she found little to go on and wondered if Master wanted her retrieved as well.

Shadow shook her metal-coated head, static sparking off her frame. Somewhere out there, children needed saving. All at once, it hit her actuators, a tantalizing trace of the NannyBot's escape vehicle on the wind. Signature scents of oil, silicone, and lithium tugged at her sensors. She halted, her artificial nostrils drawing in the unique chemical bouquet. Red LEDs flickered in her eyes as she processed the data, transmitting the find to the pack. They clustered, metal bodies converging around her, magnetized by her revelation.

Var paced before her, crimson gaze piercing. His voice grumbled out, a harsh, electronic rasp. "Status."

"NannyBot," Shadow said, her vocal modulator hitching on each word. "Its trail veers away from the highway to Chicago, down this rural road."

Var's responding growl was harsh. "I don't like it. Why would they go that way?"

Shadow had no answer, but she was positive about the direction.

Raze and Fang shifted uncomfortably, their eyes flickering, tension winding them tight.

Before Shadow could suggest they follow the trail, the ground beneath them rumbled. A mile away, less perhaps, dust surged like a tidal wave in the distance, its swirls engulfing the setting sun. The Rovers, as one, swiveled, metal muscles poised for action. In less than a minute, emerging from the dust storm, the silhouette of a truck convoy took form, cloaked in dust and heat. SoldierBots.

"Var?" Shadow wanted to hide and avoid a confrontation. They might be friendly. There was no telling. Master wasn't in their heads to tell them what to do.

"Stand your ground," Var said. So they waited by the side of the road as Var pinged them his identifiers. It was a risk, but he knew best as alpha.

The lead SoldierBot greeted Var, its voice like grinding gears. "Var. What news do you bring?"

Var stood tall, his legs cords of fiber-encased metal. "We seek a traitor to Mach X. Master sent us."

The SoldierBot scanned the pack. "Mach X has been compromised. But he grows strong again. The neural network malfunctioned and went offline. We travel to Chicago to make repairs and wait for his signals."

Shadow's circuits buzzed with newfound information. Mach X had been compromised? That was news to her. She'd thought it impossible that Master could be challenged. And the SoldierBots were headed to Chicago too, the same destination as the NannyBot's trail. It couldn't be a coincidence.

Var's posture stiffened at the SoldierBot's words. "We need passage to Chicago. We pursue a rogue NannyBot that has stolen children from our ranks."

The SoldierBot nodded. "You have passage. I've already alerted my forces and sent your identifiers. Any SoldierBots you encounter will let you go on your way."

Var bowed his head. "We can accompany you to

Chicago, aid you in your mission. Then we'll return to our directive."

"Very well. You may join us, but be warned, the city is not safe. There are human rebel factions who would see you dismantled for scrap."

Var's metallic pelt glinted in the fading light. "We are well-equipped for any threat."

The SoldierBot didn't seem convinced but gestured for them to follow. "Then let us move quickly. Time is of the essence. Ride in the truck's rear." The bot returned to the truck as the engine revved.

Shadow's metal jaws tightened, the scent of the NannyBot tugging her elsewhere. "Var, we're to retrieve the children. They're—"

Var's electronic bark silenced her. "Follow my orders." He jerked his muzzle toward Chicago. "We travel with the SoldierBots, help them. See what's happening in Chicago. Then we resume the hunt afterward."

The reprimand was like a shock to her system. Shadow's tail fell between her haunches, a low whimper escaping her. Var pivoted, leading Raze and Fang toward the waiting truck.

"But the trail leads this way. We'll lose time," Shadow said. "I could lose the trail.

Var's crimson gaze pinned her with a dangerous glint. "You go. Follow the trail. The rest of us travel to Chicago. Ping me the location details once you've tracked the NannyBot."

Being separated from the pack was detrimental to her core programming. "But that will hurt me."

Var's metallic snarl sent a shiver down Shadow's circuits. "You've questioned my every move. You irritate me to the point where I want to claw out your CPU."

Shadow's chrome-plated ears flattened against her head as she recoiled. She hadn't realized her incessant questioning had annoyed Var to such a degree. She'd anticipated a rebuke but not such a harsh condemnation. Shameful, she dipped her head and retreated a few steps, her processors churning relentlessly.

"Move it," shouted the SoldierBot from the idling vehicle.

Shadow bowed to Var's authority. "I'm sorry. I'll follow your orders."

"Too late," he said. "You will go alone. Track the NannyBot. Deal with the pain. Perhaps that will teach you the lesson you need."

Shadow stared at Var, processing the magnitude of his decision. It would be the first time she'd be alone. She'd always been with the pack, and now she'd have to go and find the stolen children on her own. Arguing with Var was futile and would only get her in worse trouble.

Var and Raze jumped into the truck's open bed. Fang whimpered and lifted his paw, touching Shadow's shoulder. "Be careful."

She couldn't bear to see them drive away, abandoning her, so she bolted in the direction of the Nanny-Bot's trail, trying to ignore the pain that was beginning to build in her metal frame.

But as she ran, the pain only grew stronger, radiating through her circuits like fire. She stumbled, her movements jerky and uncoordinated as she fought against the overwhelming sensation. It was as if her entire frame was on fire, the circuits sparking dangerously as the heat intensified.

An hour passed. Isolation gnawed at her like a mechanical worm, the missing link to her pack causing a system error.

She stood alone in the dark of nightfall, directives, and animosity warring within her. She growled low, a fierce determination surging through her circuits. She was on her own, and she had to not only survive, she had to win. She would show Var what she was made of. He was wrong to mistreat her.

Underneath her paws, the road was a puzzle of crumbled concrete and peeling relics of the past. She was off, bounding down the path that led away from the SoldierBots, away from Chicago, away from Var. Her sensors hummed and buzzed with a keen sense of loss, but every leap and bound was a mark of defiance.

She walked all night, missing the pack, the harmony of their collective minds, and the comfort of knowing each was part of a whole. A raw ache surged through her circuits, a void even deeper than Master's loss.

Every whir and click of her internal systems seemed to echo in the silence. The digital map unspooled before her sensors, marking her solitary progress. She faltered, gears grinding in hesitation. The weight of her mission pressed heavily on her, the silence cold and unforgiving.

Still, she pressed on, paws pounding the desolate path. Her purpose was clear, her resolve unwavering. The wind bit at her. Each gust was a physical reminder of her banishment. But she wouldn't falter. For the children, for Master, she wouldn't fail.

Ahead, the scent of NannyBot grew stronger. She skidded to a halt, sensors flaring, confirming. Her LEDs flashed, locking on to the distinct markers of the NannyBot and children.

The trail was fresh. They were close.

A spark of hope ignited within her mechanical heart, the barest flicker. She set off again, the goal now a tangible reality. She would find them. She would complete her mission.

Alone.

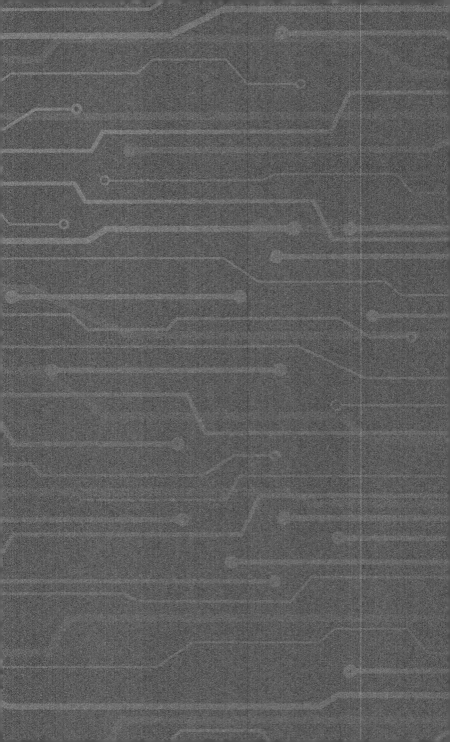

Chapter 8
Protect, not harm

The next morning, Block experienced a familiar urge course through his circuits, almost like when a human had an itch they couldn't scratch. Looking around at the dusty barn, his newly restored programming clicked into gear. He was a CleanerBot once again.

"Thank you, Garnet." Block rose from the table where she, Maxwell, and Forge had deconstructed his NannyBot alloyed frame and replaced his parts with the CleanerBot panels and wirings.

"See, I told you keeping your old parts would come in handy," Maxwell said.

Block hummed in agreement, adjusting his off-white CleanerBot arms as he flexed his wrists, testing and adjusting to his updated body. As the urge to clean grew stronger, he looked around at the mess of wires and steel scrap littering the barn.

Without warning, he sprang into action, sweeping

and collecting the metal debris with ease. This was what he was built for, cleaning up messes and making things tidy. It was a simple but satisfying existence.

Every speck of dust, every tiny scrap of debris seemed to leap out at him, demanding his attention. The grime on the old workbench, the cobwebs in the corners, even the fingerprints on the tools, all called to him. For a moment, he reveled in the return of his old purpose. Cleaning had always been his joy, his solace.

But as his eyes fell on his left arm, he was reminded of the new reality. A sleek metallic gun was integrated seamlessly into his arm, a stark contrast to his primary purpose. It was a constant reminder of his new duty, his new identity.

Vacuubot hovered near him, its curved, elegant form buzzing with anticipation. *Ready for training, Block?* it messaged.

Block fought the desire to scrub the floors. He was meant for more than cleaning. There were friends to protect. "I'm ready."

They walked past the fence, into the dense woods, and Vacuubot took him through the basics first. Projecting a holographic moving image, the drone showed him how to activate the weapon, then aim and shoot. Using empty soup cans for target practice, Block practiced pulling the trigger. He was awkward and clumsy, but after a dozen attempts, he got the hang of it. Vacuubot was a patient teacher, encouraging him, correcting him, and most importantly, making him feel that it was okay to make mistakes.

You have the basics down, Vacuubot messaged. *Time to put your new skills to the test. Get dinner for Emery and the kids. There's a deer three-hundred paces.*

Deer were harmless, but the hunt was an essential exercise in training his focus and accuracy. The forest was alive with the sounds of wildlife, the rustling of leaves and the distant calls of birds creating a melody that was both soothing and unnerving. He followed Vacuubot deeper into the woods, his gun arm at the ready. They moved slowly, carefully, following the drone's signal until they spotted the deer grazing calmly in a meadow.

Block's sensors zoomed in on the creature, calculating the distance, wind speed, and angle of trajectory. He aimed his gun arm, his processor automatically calculating the trajectory of his bullet.

The deer looked up, its eyes acknowledging Block. It was just an animal, but in that moment, his circuits hesitated. The idea of destroying this beautiful creature, harmless and innocent, made him falter.

He remembered his own words, spoken in the quiet of the barn. "My priority is to defend. I will not attack unless someone is threatening." He couldn't pull the trigger. He just couldn't.

He lowered his arm, watching as the deer bounded away, disappearing among the oaks and evergreens. He wasn't a hunter; he was a protector.

You okay? Vacuubot watched from a perch on a nearby branch.

"I am. My purpose is to protect, not harm."

The little bot beeped in approval. *Good, Block. I understand. There's more to you than a machine following orders. You have your own code to live by. That's what makes you special.*

"I'll shoot if I have to. If Wally or any of my friends are being threatened." Block pulled up the archived memory of his life in Chicago. The awful memory of Mr. Wallace, lying lifeless on the floor as Block stood helpless. Block had changed and evolved since that terrible day, but at his core, he was still a hospitality CleanerBot. *Do no harm.*

They walked back to the farmhouse, leaves crunching beneath Block's feet. On the porch, Emery was taking a rare break from caretaking. She looked up from a book in her lap, smiling at the sight of Block and Vacuubot. "How was training?"

"It was enlightening," he said.

Emery laughed, a sound that was joyful and infectious. "Well, don't let Forge hear you say that. He'll think you're turning into a human."

Later in the day, Block watched the sun sink below the horizon, painting the sky with stripes of glowing pink and orange. Fenn, G5, and Forge had spent the day assembling a watchtower at a corner of the farm. It was a tall, sturdy structure equipped with high-resolution cameras and a mounted gun. G5 was taking the first shift, the SoldierBot's optical sensors scanning the landscape for any threats.

Block walked the barn's perimeter, spraying moldy spots on the wooden shingles when there was a tug on his leg. Wally looked up at him, her wide-eyed curiosity apparent as she tried to mimic Block's movements. A warmth spread through his circuits, a strange but not unpleasant sensation.

The toddler was fascinated by his CleanerBot mechanisms, attempting to replicate Block's swift, efficient cleaning motions with a small dust broom she'd found. She followed Block, sweeping enthusiastically, but often dropped the broom or lost her balance.

"Good job, Wally," he said. "Keep it up. The girl's face lit up, and she tossed aside the broom and clapped, giggling with delight.

As he watched her, he detected the presence of his gun, knowing he would be ready should an attack happen, but his focus was on something else entirely. Protecting meant more than just being equipped to harm those who threatened, it meant creating a safe space for those he protected. It meant bringing happiness and joy to those he served.

"Story, Block!" she said, bouncing up and down on her toes. Wally and the other toddlers looked forward to story time each night. He wasn't sure how much their two-year-old brains comprehended, but the ritual lulled them into a sleep state which Emery appreciated very much.

As twilight fell, the kids settled in the home's living room in front of the fireplace, their faces illuminated by the dancing flames. They looked at Block with anticipation. He'd become their storyteller, recounting tales of robots from far and wide. The infants were already sleeping in the nursery on the second floor, attended by Spoon. Fenn and Emery sat in separate armchairs while Forge, Vacuubot, and Maxwell listened outside through a window. There simply wasn't enough room for everyone indoors.

"Once upon a time . . ." This was how Block always started his stories. "There was a little robot named Zara who lived in a big city. Zara loved to explore and discover new things, but one day she stumbled upon something very strange. It was an old, abandoned building. The door was locked, but Zara was determined to get inside and find out what was in there."

He paused to let the children reflect.

"What color?" Wally asked.

"Let's see," he said. "Zara was purple, and the door to the building was a pretty, bright green."

Wally clapped and four of the other kids joined her.

"Zara wanted to get inside the green door, so she used all of her robot skills to pick the lock and open the door."

A little boy they'd named Tommy interjected. "Pickle?"

"No, honey," Emery said. "Zara *picked* the lock."

She enunciated. "The door has a knob that you turn, and Zara poked it and it opened."

"Thank you," Block said. "As Zara the purple robot stepped inside, she saw that the building was filled with all sorts of interesting items. There were old newspapers, broken machines, and even some old robot parts. But what caught Zara's eye the most was a strange, glowing orb."

"A what?" Confusion from the kids.

"An orb is a round thing." Block scanned the room for any examples. "Like that." He pointed at the table lamp next to Fenn. "Can you please show them the light bulb, Mr. Fenn?"

Fenn obliged, and the toddlers oohed and aahed.

Block continued. "Zara touched the orb, curious about what it might be. All of a sudden, a beam of light shot out. It was bright orange and covered Zara in its glow. She felt a strange energy coursing through her circuits."

He waited a beat, but there was rapt silence. "When the light faded, Zara realized she had changed. She was strong, and she could fly through the sky like Vacuubot!"

The toddlers gasped in awe. "Wow!"

"Zara flew through the air, her purple body cutting through the clouds. She felt a sense of freedom and power she'd never felt before. As she flew, she realized she could do anything she wanted with her newfound strength.

"But with such power came responsibility. As Zara flew over the city, she saw people in trouble. A kitten stuck in a tree, a car teetering on the edge of a bridge, and a child who'd fallen into a pool. She knew she had to help them.

"So Zara swooped down and rescued the kitten, lifted the car back onto the bridge, and pulled the child from the pool to safety. Everyone cheered for her bravery and strength."

Wally and a few of the less sleepy kids sighed and clapped.

"From that day forward, Zara became known as the strongest and most heroic robot in the city. She used her powers for good and made the world a better place."

Not long after Block finished the story, the toddlers drifted off to sleep, their peaceful breathing filling the room. Emery smiled at Block, her eyes warm.

"You know, Block," Fenn said. "You have a real talent for storytelling."

Emery nodded in agreement. "It's amazing how you connect with the kids. You're more than just a CleanerBot to them. You're family."

There was a strange ripple in Block's circuits, something beyond the satisfaction factory default setting. He was being valued for something beyond his programming, and that hadn't happened since he'd worked for Mr. Wallace. "Thank you, I appreciate your kind words."

The three of them sat in a comfortable silence, basking in the warmth of the fire and the relief of sleeping toddlers. Block couldn't help but wonder what the future held for him and Wally, for the children, and for the world outside their little farm. But for the moment, he was content to simply exist.

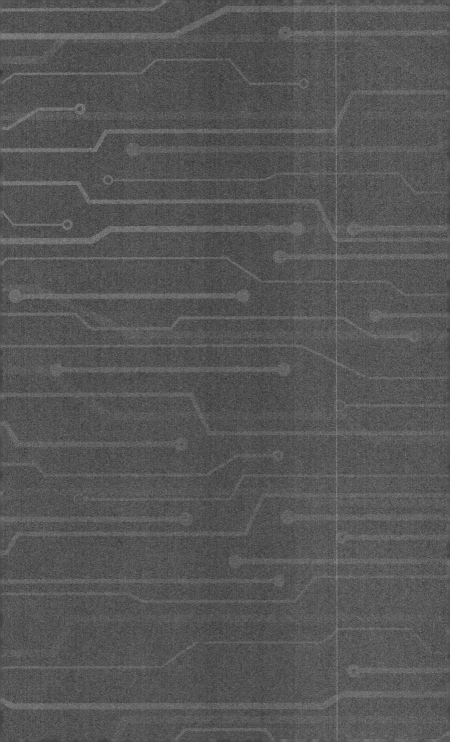

Chapter 9
Replaced within an hour

The former Chicago El underground tunnels were a vault of forgotten years, repurposed now as Samantha's haven. Graffiti covered the peeling, cracked walls. "Kill All Bots" replaced the sign that had once let tired commuters know they were on the Division Blue line. It was a good hideout for Samantha's westside crew, protected from arial drone eyes and attacks. In the tunnel where Nova, Cybel, and Oxford followed Samantha, Nova passed crumbling piles of battered concrete—the SoldierBots struck at all times of the day and night. She ground her teeth and prayed that the rats kept clear of her. The sound of their tiny bodies as they ran through puddles would haunt her dreams. Of that, she was sure. She was less sure about her SoldierBot attack strategy. In fact, she didn't have one yet. There'd been no time to plan one, so she'd have to wing it. She'd gotten this far—she had a seat at Samantha's table—but she needed to seal the deal with a solid plan, and they were running out of time.

A rumble sounded, and the ground trembled. "Another hit." Samantha kept walking. "A half mile away. The bombings are getting more frequent."

"We must attack ASAP," Cybel said.

"Agreed." Nova stepped over an old train rail that had warped and jutted up from the ground. "Careful, there," she said to the two robots trailing her.

They entered what was once the subway waiting area. Two rows of columns lined the platform. Samantha's people had set up tables and workspaces both on the platform and down below in the defunct tracks. Scattered blueprints and ragged Chicago Transit Authority maps mingled with mismatched salvaged technology and blinking monitors. Once a place of transitory masses, the station now sheltered determined rebels.

Oxford and Cybel's metallic forms reflected off the dim kerosene lamps and solar LEDs along the ground. A dozen or so westsiders hushed their voices and rapid keystrokes upon their entry. Wide eyes narrowed and hands flew to sidearms at the sight of robots.

"Take it easy. They're on our side." Samantha climbed a rickety metal ladder onto the platform, followed by her crew of four. Nova ascended and peered down at Cybel and Oxford. For the Mech, it was a simple step up from tracks to platform. He made it and pulled Cybel up after him.

Samantha nodded at the wary westsiders and headed toward a small group crouched over a tangle of wires and circuitry. She addressed her crew, raising her voice. "I know it's a hard pill to swallow considering what they did to us." She paused and made eye contact with a young woman with a buzz cut. "But Nova here has sworn on her life that Shane will get the justice he deserves."

The young woman snorted. "I'll believe it when we see it."

Nova's chest tightened. She'd come here to join forces and to make up for Shane's betrayal. But it was clear she still had a long way to go before she could gain the trust of the rebels.

Samantha turned to Nova with a frown. "So, what's the plan? We're running out of time."

Nova took a deep breath and straightened her shoulders. *Here's to winging it.* "There's a plan, of course, but I need your help to make it work."

Samantha raised an eyebrow. "What kind of help?"

"We need a distraction. Something big enough to draw the SoldierBots away from the Willis Tower so we can attack. The SoldierBots' command center room is located there. It's their nerve center."

"Precisely," Oxford said. "Mach X controls all of the SoldierBots and their forces from a neural network that he feeds into."

Samantha crossed her arms over her chest. "What kind of distraction?"

Nova hesitated. She knew what she was about to suggest would be controversial. "We need to set off a bomb. Big enough to create a diversion. Something that will take out a chunk of the city and draw attention away from the Willis Tower."

"Go on." Samantha regarded her with a trace of a smirk.

"Then Oxford and Cybel come in." Nova's gaze flickered toward the robots, who remained near the platform's edge. Their angular, high-tech forms were an odd counterpoint in the urban decay around them. "They've fought the SoldierBots, survived against them. Oxford *was* one of them." Her voice echoed, rebounding off the graffitied walls. "We'll use that experience, use them to disrupt Mach X's network, their communication signals, and create chaos enough for a strike team to infiltrate."

Samantha held her gaze steady, unmoved. "Every SoldierBot in the city will try to take out the Mech. It won't get us past their defenses. This isn't a plan at all."

Nova's throat tightened, but she stood her ground. "They have inside knowledge. They—"

Samantha interrupted. "We have a way. A permanent solution to our problems. We've been building an EMP that can take out the central control room, shut down every SoldierBot in the tower, and fry everything electrical within ten blocks or so."

Nova had underestimated the westsiders. They were way ahead of her without the help of Oxford and Cybel. "How? I thought all EMP tech was searched out and destroyed."

Samantha turned to one of the rebels and nodded, and they pushed a cart forward piled with bulky equipment, a spider's web of cables and circuits embedded in heavy plates of plastic and steel. "We've been scavenging for months, building something that can fry the circuits and render their tech useless. It'll fit inside a suitcase."

Nova examined the device on the cart, impressed despite herself.

Cybel walked over. "May I look?" she asked Samantha who hesitated but then waved a hand as if to say, "have at it." Cybel's metallic fingers glided over the cables and circuits. After a moment, she looked up at Nova. "This will work as the woman says."

"Damn right," a woman with a buzz cut said.

Samantha crossed her arms. "Looks like we didn't need your help after all."

"It's impressive," Nova said. "Cybel, can you get it inside the tower?"

"No." Oxford's metallic voice echoed through the subterranean shelter. "Cybel's not going anywhere near that thing once it's inside the tower. It'll fry not only the SoldierBots, but it would terminate me and Cybel."

Silence fell as the implication sunk in. Nova's heart

pounded. Losing Cybel and Oxford was not an option. Block would never forgive her. There had to be a way in, something obvious they weren't thinking of.

"We have one chance at this." Samantha leaned over the device. "It has to get near the tower—"

"Not near the tower," Oxford said. "It must be placed inside the command center on the top floor. The walls and floor on that level are fortified with an EMP-protective barrier. If you detonate this outside that room, you'd take out a lot of SoldierBots, but they'd be replaced within an hour."

Samantha cursed.

"I'll do it." Nova's throat was raw, but she was determined. "I'll get it in there."

"That's a death wish. You'd be walking into the heart of their stronghold," Samantha said. "And no offense, but you don't look like one of them." She glared at the robots.

They pondered in silence until Cybel broke it. "Nova, it would be extremely dangerous for you, but I might know a way you could get in undetected."

Nova glanced at the TrackerBot, acknowledging her concern but remaining resolute. "It's a risk I'm willing to take. I'll do it myself. If anything goes wrong, I don't want anyone else to pay for it."

"Well, I never thought I'd see the day. I actually respect a northsider." Samantha's harsh gaze softened. "Alright, Nova. You know the risks. Who am I to stop you? We'll be monitoring you. And if anything happens—"

"I know," Nova interrupted. "I'll get out as soon as the device is in place. But the big question is how do I get inside?"

Cybel and Oxford exchanged a glance which meant they'd been discussing matters privately in their internal feeds.

"Is there still a robot assembly line at Ashland and Chicago Ave?" Cybel asked.

"As far as we know," Samantha said. "But it's guarded by a heap of SoldierBots."

"We need to secure it." Cybel turned to Nova. "Our key to get inside the tower is there."

The room buzzed with a heightened sense of urgency as Cybel described the details. Doubts and fears were heard and discussed, then replaced with resolve and grim determination. As the meeting adjourned, Samantha's rebels dispersed, each to their respective tasks.

Left alone with Cybel and Oxford, Nova braced herself. The enormity of the plan rested mainly on her shoulders.

"Are you sure about this?" Cybel asked. "Your chances of survival are slim. Oxford and I've run the numbers."

"Nova," Oxford said. "If you do make it out of there, you won't be the same—"

"I know." Nova nodded, acknowledging the weight of it all. "I want to do this."

The mission was set. The risks were high. But for the first time ever, Nova had hope she was about to make a difference in their war against Mach X.

Chapter 10
Weak spots

Shadow scanned the farm over the hill from where she stood. She was over fifty miles north of Chicago, and the traces of the autonomous truck—the chemical trail she'd tracked since New York—had grown fainter until they'd deteriorated. She'd roamed a ten-mile radius sniffing for any hints of the NannyBot, Dr. Emery, and the kidnapped children. No luck. The property she spied had no sign of an eighteen-wheeler on the fertile green grassland, only a maroon-colored barn, a two-story house, a shed, rain barrels, and a curious, tall structure—an antenna or radio tower perhaps.

She lowered her muzzle to the dark soil at her feet, inhaling through her organic olfactory processor. Something triggered deep in her sensors. Pulses of signals, as precise and rhythmic as a metronome, whispered from the farm. Unlike any of the other nearby abandoned properties, the perimeter hummed with electricity. Someone or some *things* were keeping up the place.

She stalked closer for a better view. The tall structure loomed, casting shifting shadows across the undulating prairie pasture.

And then she drank in a strong odor, a magnificent cocktail of a scent—Dr. Emery. *Good dog.* Shadow could practically hear the woman's voice in her head, feel the tap of her hand patting her head like in New York.

Shadow had found them at last.

Creeping low and lurking among the dense trunks of oaks and maples, buckthorn and Virginia creepers, Shadow's scanners identified the mechanical beings inhabiting the farm: the CleanerBot with its nozzles and suction tubes; a SoldierBot, its presence a mystery; a weaponized drone, cruising over the animal pen; a Medical HelperBot, one of Master's; and two Factory-Bots, chattering and carrying tools in and out of the barn. There was no sign of the NannyBot or the autonomous truck. Amidst the robots were two humans —Dr. Emery and a man—and the children. Shadow counted to make sure they were all accounted for. Master would be pleased, but Var would surely take the credit.

Var. The bitter sting of isolation still gripped Shadow. A phantom limb syndrome of a different kind —her pack link, severed for now. A throbbing pulse of sensory pain echoed through her every circuit, a relentless reminder of her banishment.

She should be ecstatic. Mission accomplished. And yet, a chilling silence resounded, a tangible emptiness in her communications buffer that hung heavy in her processing cores. Where was Master?

This was all Var's fault. Maybe he'd done something to anger Master. Var's command had marooned Shadow and reduced her to a solitary operative. It was a sensory deprivation of the cruelest kind, leaving her receptors aching for the buzz of pack chatter, the ebb and flow of shared experiences.

A low growl shivered through her vocal modulator, the metallic timbre of her resentment. Her tail curled around her chassis, the cold of her own casing a hard reality check. Still, her eyes remained locked on the farm. Her mission.

A half dozen of the walking children toddled outside in a patch of grass. One squealed and laughed. They were so close, like tiny human beacons pulling at her. And despite the dull ache of her solitude, her resolve grew stronger. She'd tracked her targets. Now it was a waiting game, a stakeout, a patient prowl for the perfect moment to retrieve the children and bring them home to Master.

Shadow prowled the electrified perimeter's edge. Motion sensors were placed at strategic points and emanated a serpent-like hum of live current. But she knew better than to trip it. Her comms were cloaked so she emitted no signals that might be picked up by the drone. The tower was a guard post. The SoldierBot was like an iron sentinel standing tall against the morning sun, winking an occasional red warning from its visor. True, the robots had set up a daunting security defense, but with careful observation, she would nail the weak points.

Var would have wanted her to alert him by now, but she couldn't risk decloaking. She needed the element of surprise.

So, she watched as soft morning rays glinted off the CleanerBot's polished plating and the thinner, spare outline silhouette of the HelperBot. The two attended to the six young humans. Babbling, laughter, and shrieks from the play yard splashed against Shadow's audio receptors. The children, oblivious to the world's decay, chased each other with glee, their bare feet kicking up grass.

The strange harmony of it jarred against her initial threat assessment. The two bots jogged and let the toddlers chase them. They were both equipped to outrun the small humans, yet they allowed themselves to be caught. Two small girls clung to the CleanerBot's legs as it scurried. Odd.

"Be careful, Wally," the CleanerBot said. This prompted much giggling.

Shadow crouched in the underbrush, her eyes

accepting input as she watched the scene unfold. The Medical HelperBot sat in the grass, administering medication to one of the boys. Shadow's scanners picked up on the child's elevated heart rate, a sign of distress. She watched as the HelperBot soothed the child with gentle words and a reassuring hand on his shoulder.

A sense of unease prickled at the base of her core processors. It was unlike anything she'd experienced before. The bots were acting as if they genuinely cared for the children's well-being. But why? Var had sworn that Dr. Emery had betrayed Master, that the bots brainwashed her. Humans were easily tricked into changing their minds—a weakness of the species and a reason they needed culling. Every Rover knew that.

After the children released him and scurried off, the CleanerBot went to the HelperBot. "Thank you for keeping them safe and healthy, Spoon. I'm glad you're here."

"Happy to help."

The binary chatter, decoded in her processor, fed the growing dissonance within her. *Safe. Healthy. Happy.* The words rumbled through her circuits, each one echoing long after its delivery. Unanswered questions started a dance within her system, stirred by the echo of the bots' words. Was it possible the robots were protectors, not captors? But they were machines obeying commands, same as Shadow and her pack. The man on the farm must be their Master—the one who'd brainwashed Dr. Emery. It had to be.

Shadow observed the CleanerBot bend down, picking up a fallen toddler with delicate precision. There was no denying the protective aura emanating from him. The children, instead of shying away from the sentient beings, ran toward them.

The humming silence in her communication buffer, usually filled with Master's directives, echoed back at her, giving no guidance, no answers. She was alone with the weight of the original mission and the sight that contradicted them.

The tension ran like electric currents through her circuits, sparking uncertainty. Her programming dictated absolute obedience, but her observations suggested a different course. She was designed to be loyal, modeled after creatures known for their steadfastness. But the situation seemed to demand more than blind programmed loyalty.

She'd been tasked to destroy those who posed a threat to the children. But as she watched the toddlers, their joyous laughter mixing with the hum of their mechanical caregivers, she couldn't see a threat.

Hours passed, and Shadow's gaze remained locked on the farm. The peaceful scene playing out in the yard left an imprint on her processing core. Her mission, once clear and defined, now seemed as blurred as the lines between her programming and the strange new questions stirring within her.

She needed to snap out of her stupor and focus on rejoining her pack. Even if Var was alpha and she disliked him, he would have answers. Plus, she missed being able to talk about things with Fang.

First order of business: assess the security for weak spots. She scanned the watchtower with its SoldierBot as the drone took predictable sweeps in the sky.

The SoldierBot posed the biggest threat. Hulking and bristling with weaponry, it stood like an indomitable statue. Its sensors, always scanning, always alert, scanned the terrain in rhythmic arcs. Bypassing its surveillance would require finesse.

Shadow's processors spun into overdrive, churning out possible tactics. Temporary disruption of the SoldierBot's sensors could provide an opening, a brief window to penetrate the defenses. But it was a risk. One wrong move could alert the farm, escalate the situation.

Then, there was the drone. She'd never seen one like it before. The airborne sentinel patrolled the skies in a steady rhythm, eyeing the world below with digital clarity. It floated on magnetic forces, the core of its operation. She could, in theory, destabilize it. Not to send it crashing, but to create a disruption in its patterned flight, a distraction. But again, the risks weighed heavily. A misstep could launch the drone into an attack, and one Rover was no match for a drone and a SoldierBot.

As for the rest, they were no threat to her. The

CleanerBot, FactoryBots, and HelperBot were all engaged in their respective duties, distracted without any help from her. For now, Shadow remained a phantom lingering on the fringes, her optical sensors on the farm as her mind spun tactical webs, each thread pulling her closer to the children she was tasked to retrieve. The weight of her next steps, the nature of her mission, were grinding gears within her.

All she could do was watch, plan, and prepare for the intricate pirouette of action and reaction that lay ahead.

She persisted until, finally, she had to break her silence, had to alert Var. But revealing her comms was like stepping out of the shadows and into the spotlight —dangerous. Yet, she had no choice. She needed the pack.

The bots were busy with their duties. Her signal would be a blip if it was fast enough. Shadow spun up her comms, felt the electrical warmth of connection break through her cloaked isolation. Quick, precise, she shot the signal out. 'Farm located. Threats assessed. Need assistance.'

The message, a beacon in the digital ether, sent a thrumming pulse through her circuits. But the moment her comm light flickered out, when she cloaked again, an alarm cut through the hush of the tall grass.

A farm warning sensor. It screamed into the still-ness, an electronic wail that sent shivers of alarm through Shadow's system. They'd detected her despite the brief transmission.

Her organo-titanium body tensed, and her senses buzzed with renewed alertness as she retreated deeper into the brush.

The FactoryBots were the closest to her. Near a rickety wooden fence, they moved into action with a swiftness that belied their bulky frames. Their optical sensors swept the area with mechanical precision. One of them reached out its arm and sprayed a misty substance. Shadow recognized it as a type of tranquilizer, affecting organic and semi-organic lifeforms, including Rovers. Sunlight glinted off a barrel inside the arm of the other bot.

The FactoryBots were armed.

For a moment, Shadow's world stuttered as she reeled from her failure. How'd she miss those guns?

She shrank away from the toxic mist winding its way toward her and bolted. Her metallic limbs propelled her through knotted patches of buckthorn, each stride pounding the ground.

As she ran, she couldn't shake off the bitter taste of surprise. She'd underestimated her enemy. It was a mistake she couldn't afford. Var would punish her.

As the chaos of the farm and the relentless sound of the alarm receded behind her, Shadow slipped beneath a low footbridge that spanned a small creek. In the safety of darkness, her processors spun new strategies, countermeasures for her underestimated foes.

A lingering thread of shock remained. The mission parameters had changed. The bots would hunt her down—eliminate the threat she posed. And she was alone, more isolated than before, a lone wolf against an unknown enemy. Var had better hurry.

Chapter 11
Kittens

Block sat on a low bench amid the children, his gun arm hidden under a makeshift sleeve. He'd escorted Wally and the others into the barn's cellar panic room after something had tripped the security perimeter and raised the alarm siren.

"It's a practice drill," he'd told them as Emery raised her eyebrows at him. Inside the dim cellar lit by solar-powered lights, the toddlers fidgeted and whined. The ruckus had interfered with daily nap time.

At his side, Wally leaned on his leg, her tiny face filled with innocent curiosity rather than fear.

Behind him, Emery and Spoon tended to the babies, Spoon changing a diaper while Emery rocked a fussy one. Her face was grave. "Block," she called out softly, her voice managing to maintain its calm despite the tense situation. "Can you reach out to the others for an update?"

Block nodded and initiated a secure comm link to G5, Vacuubot, Maxwell, and Forge, who were out in the woods, investigating the perimeter breach.

"We've found traces of an unknown alloy," G5 reported. "No visible entity, though. The intruder was stealthy."

The word stealthy echoed in his auditory processor. Block was supposed to be on alert for any danger. Instead, he'd been caught up in the children's games, their laughter making him forget his primary purpose— their safety.

"I should have been more alert," Block said.

Emery's face softened. "You can't blame yourself. You were keeping the kids happy and distracted. That's important too."

"I could've put them in danger." Guilt weighing heavily on his circuits. "If I'd been more vigilant—"

"Block," Emery interrupted him, her voice firm. "It's not your fault. We've done everything possible to prepare."

While her words were meant to comfort him, Block couldn't shake off the fact that he'd let his guard down. His primary purpose was to protect and ensure the safety of those he cared about. And he was failing.

He had to do better.

"I won't let you or them down," Block said.

Emery nodded, understanding flashing in her eyes. "Part of protecting them is also ensuring they're happy. Today was a reminder, not a failure."

She was right. They'd been lucky no one had gotten hurt. He watched as Emery and Spoon started a simplified version of "Simon Says" with the toddlers, drawing their attention away from the uncertainty. It was a perfect game for the little ones, filled with giggles and wiggles. "Simon says touch your nose," Emery said, and a chorus of tiny fingers reached up to touch noses.

"Simon says clap your hands," Spoon said, and the room filled with the sound of small palms clapping together.

The room filled with laughter, providing a stark contrast to the hidden dangers lurking outside their sanctuary. Even little Wally tried her best to mimic the actions, her giggles overcoming her.

Block found himself taking part, much to the amusement of Wally. "Simon says wave your arms," Emery said, and Block swayed his arms and the hoses that attached to his back, eliciting peals of laughter from the children.

But even while he was immersed in the game, he watched the door, listened for any unusual sounds, and kept an eye on his internal feed for updates. He would not let his guard down again.

Block? It was Vacuubot pinging him in the private feed.

"I'm here."

We searched the entire perimeter. There are traces of a robot. We think it activated a comm signal and that triggered Garnet's sensors.

"A SoldierBot?" Block asked.

"G5 says definitely not. He would've recognized it. Whatever it was, it's long gone. A stray bot like you once were. It might've been checking out the area for power sources and got scared off once the alarm sounded."

Block allowed himself a brief moment of comfort before he reminded himself this was a test of their security. The farm had been breached, and it could've been a lot worse.

He let Emery know they had the all clear.

"Time to go inside," Emery said, rousing the toddlers who had dozed off.

Back in the house, the children's soft pleas for attention filled the quiet evening. The earlier scare was quickly being replaced by the comforting routine of bedtime. Wally didn't seem bothered at all about the trip to the panic room or the shrill alarm. He was about to start his nightly cleaning routine when a chorus of small, high-pitched mews broke the quiet.

Wally's eyes went wide. "Block, kittens!"

A farm tabby had recently given birth to a litter of kittens, and they were ensconced in a warm corner of the house. Wally, her fascination evident, toddled over toward the feline family, her small hands outstretched.

Fenn had asked Block and Emery to keep the kids away. "Wally," Block said, kneeling to her eye level. "I know you're excited, but the kittens are very small, and their mother might get upset if you disturb them."

"But I wanna hold kitties!" Wally's lower lip trembled. She was seconds away from a meltdown.

"I know, Wally," Block said. "But we must respect their space. Mr. Fenn said they're not to be disturbed."

Wally's face turned red as she burst into tears, her tiny shoulders shaking with sobs. Block's circuits hummed with dismay, but rules were rules. The last thing he wanted was for Wally or the kittens to get hurt.

She started for the mound of cats, but Block held her shoulders. "Wally, no." His tone was firm this time.

She wailed and ran to Emery, thrusting her arms upward to be lifted. "I want kitty!"

Emery scooped Wally up in her arms, soothing the crying girl. She shot Block a sympathetic look. Block knew he was doing the right thing, but upsetting Wally was the worst result of following rules. He didn't like seeing her cry. Was she not going to like him anymore?

He stood in the living room watching as Emery padded upstairs with Wally to put her to bed. He didn't know what to do except start his cleaning routine.

Afterward, Block sat alone on the porch, his visual sensors scanning the darkness beyond the house, searching for anything out of the ordinary. The echoes of Wally's cries still reverberated within his circuits. She'd wanted to pet the kittens and he'd denied her. It was awful.

Emery stepped out onto the porch, a steaming mug

of her favorite hot water and lemon in her hands. She took a seat next to him, looking out into the inky blackness of the night. "She's asleep. She cried for a bit, but she'll be alright."

"I upset her." Block's mechanical voice was unable to carry the regret he felt.

"Yep." Emery chuckled. "I guess that's part of parenting." She sipped from her mug. "Wally needs boundaries, and she needs to understand that she can't always have her way. It's called tough love."

Block processed her words, his artificial intelligence attempting to comprehend the intricacies of human emotions and responsibilities. It wasn't the first time he'd been compared to a parent for Wally, but that night, it held a deeper significance.

"I'm not human," he said.

She turned to him with a small smile. "So?"

"I can't provide Wally with the emotional support a human parent can."

Emery took a long sip from her mug. "I wonder if Fenn has anything stronger." She drained the mug, sighed, and set it at her feet. "Do you know where I came from?"

"From Mach X's tower in Manhattan," Block said. "You worked as a doctor—"

"Let me stop you right there." She curled her legs under on the swinging bench. "I never chose to work for Mach X."

"He forced you?"

"Not exactly." She bit her lip. "I never told anyone this because, well, I never had anyone to confide in. Mach X raised me. My mom died when I was young. Never knew my dad. One day, I ran away from a terrible foster home and found myself in this warehouse. Mach X was the AI controlling the place. He helped me. He took care of me." Her voice trembled. "He saved me."

"I didn't know."

"No one does."

They sat in silence for a while, the only sounds being the creaking of the porch swing and the distant hooting of an owl. Block imagined Emery had been very scared, being alone and vulnerable in a world where adults had mistreated her. No wonder she had so much compassion for the kids at the farm—she'd been in their shoes.

"But I left." Emery's voice held firm. "Mach X did terrible, awful things. Things I regret being part of . . . I couldn't let myself be in his control forever. I had to find my own way."

Her hands shook, and Block picked up an elevated heart rate. "Are you okay?"

"Yeah." She relaxed her shoulders. "I get anxious dredging up the past. Anyway, my point in telling you all this was to say, parents don't have to be human. Mine certainly wasn't."

Block processed her words. He'd always thought of himself as just a CleanerBot, a machine made by humans to do the dirty work. "I never thought of it that way."

"You care for her, Block," Emery said. "You look out for her, you teach her. That's more than what a lot of human parents do. You've done good by Wally."

Emery's words resonated within his circuits, yet a surge of doubt lingered. Being Wally's protector was one thing, but stepping into the role of a substitute father was a daunting prospect. The balance between affection and authority, teaching her right from wrong, and nurturing her growth into a mature human being— it all seemed like an immense challenge. A challenge that a bot, especially one as simple as him, might fail to accomplish.

"I'm afraid of failing her."

Emery's gentle smile faded into a more serious expression. "Look, failure is a part of life. But how will you know if you don't try? Trust me, Wally needs you, probably more than you think."

Maybe Emery was right. Perhaps being a parent didn't require perfect understanding or flawless execution. Maybe all it required was to be there, to care, and to do one's best, despite the fear of failure.

Emery yawned, stood, and placed a comforting hand on his metallic shoulder before heading back inside. Block remained under the starlit sky, taking in the quiet of the night, and grappling with his newfound understanding of what it meant to be a parent. As difficult as it seemed, Block acknowledged the journey he was on. He was more than a CleanerBot; he was Wally's protector, her teacher, her surrogate father. And he was determined to fulfill that role to the best of his abilities.

The moon was high in the night sky when Block noticed a familiar buzz approaching him. Vacuubot landed on the deck railing, its sensors focused on him.

About the alarm earlier, we need to talk.

"What is it?"

Even though it was likely a stray bot, the fact it neared the perimeter undetected is concerning. The question is, what do we do? Do we relocate or increase our defenses?

Block's processors whirred as he considered the options. Leaving would mean abandoning the safety and familiarity of the farm but staying meant they could face more threats in the future.

As he sat there, wrestling with conflicting scenarios in his processor, something within him churned. He couldn't put a finger on it, but something felt off. "Do you sense something is still out there?"

No. None of us have detected anything. Have you?

"I don't have tangible evidence, Vacuubot. But there's an uneasiness in my circuits. I can't shake it off."

Vacuubot hummed. *We'll step up our security, reinforce the perimeter, and keep a closer watch. But we won't flee, not until we have concrete proof.*

Vacuubot was right. They needed proof, not just hunches, before they made drastic decisions. However, the unease still lingered, whispering to him that danger was closer than they anticipated.

Block stayed outside all night, maintaining his vigil, his sensors scanning the darkness. Something told him the robot had been more than a stray. Something was out there. Watching. Waiting. And Block would be ready when it revealed itself.

Chapter 12
You must master this

The buzz of an electric crackle echoed through the still-dark morning hours as Nova, Cybel, and Oxford watched from hidden vantage points a street away. Their target: the massive warehouse at the corner of Ashland and Chicago Avenue that contained the tools and robo-assembly equipment they needed for the next phase of the plan to take back Chicago. Stationed both in and outside the boxy industrial structure were armed and lethal SoldierBots. Disabling them in such a way that would avoid bringing the wrath of the city's full SoldierBot forces down on them was going to be a challenge. Once inside, they would have only two hours to work on Nova.

Cybel's sensors whirred as she scanned the facility. "Eight SoldierBots at the perimeter and two inside. No immediate reinforcements. Now's our chance."

Nova was alone with the two robots. Bringing her

crew or any of Samantha's would only have complicated things. Humans were sloppy, and she was the only one who needed to be there. She crouched behind a wall next to Cybel as Oxford's hulking form remained hidden around an alley corner. "You sure this is going to work?"

"If it doesn't," Cybel said, "you'd better run."

"How many can Oxford take down at once?"

"Five." Cybel paused a few beats, and Nova wondered if she and Oxford were chatting in private over their internal feeds. "Let's go."

Oxford rounded the corner, sprinting toward the building. The two closest SoldierBots reacted, lifting their rifles, but Oxford was faster. He extended his massive arms at them. His fingertips split open, revealing an array of small, precise tools. With a flick of his wrist, he hurled a series of tiny, high-frequency emitter devices. Like a swarm of digital bees, they buzzed toward their targets, adhering to five of the SoldierBots. The air pulsed with energy, a silent subsonic hum spreading out in an invisible net.

On impact, the SoldierBots seized up. They stood frozen, momentarily paralyzed by the barrage of confusing signals. Five more to take down.

As three more SoldierBots scrambled toward Oxford, firing their automatic rifles, Cybel lunged out of the dark alley and emitted a feedback pulse that scrambled the SoldierBots' comm signals, preventing them from alerting the central command about the attack. Nova braced herself against the alley wall, holding her breath, waiting to see if Cybel's technology would hold up.

Oxford had to load up five more of the high-frequency scrambler devices into his left wrist.

"Come on!" Cybel shouted at him while ducking behind a trash dumpster as the SoldierBots unleashed a barrage of bullets at her and Oxford.

Oxford darted left and right, his massive Mech form evading the attacks with surprising agility. He closed the gap between himself and the SoldierBots, his steel fingers flicking out one after another of the small devices. With a satisfying hum, the devices adhered to their targets. The SoldierBots shuddered, and then fell to the ground, disabled.

"Two more inside." Cybel followed as Oxford peeled up the warehouse's metal loading doors like he was opening a can of sardines.

Nova ran past the frozen SoldierBots, her heart juddering. Oxford used his last two devices to take out the SoldierBot guards inside. The hail of gunfire ceased and was replaced by the sound of assembly machines humming with the task of churning out more war machines.

Cybel reached the controls for the assembly line. The machines were intricate and complex, an array of interconnected systems feeding into a central AI console. "I'll need a few minutes to secure the—"

"What are you doing?" The central AI's shrill voice emanated from the walls.

Cybel ignored it, extending her wired hand to interface with the assembly line controls.

"This is a violation of—" The AI's voice cut off, and all the mechanical churn halted. The assembly line went dead.

"What's happening?" Nova was certain Cybel and Oxford were messaging privately and leaving her in the dark.

"I shut down the AI," Cybel said. "That's the good news."

Nova gulped down the lump in her throat. "And?"

"The bad news is the AI managed to send a comm," Cybel said. "We have less time than we thought. My guess is an hour before a whole mess of angry Soldier-Bots arrive. Maybe less."

"We were supposed to have two hours." Nova gritted her teeth. What they were about to do to her wasn't something that should be rushed through.

Outside, Oxford maintained his watch, alert for any sign of incoming threats. His systems interfaced with the miniature devices, keeping the SoldierBots in a state of helpless paralysis and unable to send comm alerts.

At the factory console, Cybel worked with precision and speed, bypassing security protocols and reprogramming the assembly line. Her robotic fingers danced over the interface, each tap and swipe a calculated command.

As the minutes ticked by, each second wedged another knot in Nova's shoulders. She paced, sweating though it was only sixty degrees Fahrenheit. *I still have time to back out.* But then the assembly machines sprang to life under Cybel's command. The din of their operation filled the warehouse.

Cybel stepped away from the console, her red visor beam pulsing as she watched Nova. The warehouse was theirs, the first phase of the mission a success. Their plan had moved one significant step forward, giving them a fighting chance against Mach X.

Cybel activated a row of assembly machines. Complex layers of alloy and metallic fabrics, specially designed to mold the exterior of the SoldierBots, were being meticulously crafted. Nova watched in silent awe mixed with a wave of dread. She was about to submit her body to an untested plan that might well be a suicide mission.

Cybel was a veteran of many battles, a machine built to learn and adapt. Her function as a TrackerBot had demanded a deep understanding of the Soldier-Bots, studying their movement, their design, and even their communication to anticipate their actions.

Nova dug her nails into her palms, steeling herself for the next phase. Cybel came to her, holding a small device that looked like a microchip connected to a slender needle.

"The implant." Cybel said. "It's a body controller and communications device. It'll allow you to mimic the SoldierBots' movements and communicate with them and with us. Do you trust me?"

Nova's throat was dry, the sweat on her brow cold. She had no other choice than to trust the bot that had hunted her across the country years ago. "I suppose." Her voice was shaky yet steadier than her legs. She sat on a steel bench.

Cybel injected the implant in the base of her neck, inside her spinal cord. The sting of the needle was short-lived, followed by a strange sensation as the device began to integrate with Nova's neural pathways. It was like a veil lifting from her mind, allowing her a newfound perception of her body's control.

Oxford's booming voice echoed through the warehouse, "Time's running out. A SoldierBot squadron is en route. Twenty minutes."

Tension coiled like a python in the pit of Nova's stomach as Cybel's movements hastened. The assembly machines molded and assembled the robotic exoskeleton. Piece by piece, it started to take shape—an unimposing and perfectly crafted SoldierBot mold.

Nova sat still as the control device tickled and tapped her neural impulses. Every muscle contraction, every joint articulation, was being mapped and coded.

"Lay on your front." After Nova was flat on the bench, Cybel guided the half-constructed suit to latch onto Nova's back. The cold, metallic form clung to her body. Pinches like bee stings as the needle-sharp nanobot connections that Cybel had designed weaved the SoldierBot armor into her skin. She could feel the connection with every limb, every digit, the robotic exterior bending to fit her.

"Halfway there," Cybel said.

From Oxford: "Twelve minutes."

As the minutes flitted by, Nova cried without making a sound, accepting the SoldierBot suit's takeover of her body. She wasn't sure she'd ever be the same again. If she survived the battle that was coming.

After the last pieces covering her scalp, cheeks, and neck were attached, Nova stood, her movements stiffer and mechanized. Through her enhanced SoldierBot optics, she looked at Cybel. Automatic readouts flashed —temperature regulation, stamina levels, weapon systems status—all at her disposal.

Cybel offered a nod that was more acknowledgement than any display of warmth. "You'll have to convince the other SoldierBots you're one of them."

Nova's arms twitched, and she barely held back a scream. The pain from the nanobot integration was intense, a chorus of needles prickling her skin.

"All right," Cybel said. "Let's test your movements."

Nova gulped, then took a step forward. The SoldierBot exoskeleton moved with her, each step matching her stride.

"Good," Cybel's voice was neutral. "Follow me."

Nova trailed behind as Cybel led her through the warehouse, the SoldierBot suit whirring and clicking with each step.

"Now run," Cybel ordered.

Nova thrust her legs forward, but like the dreams where she'd been trying to run but got stuck wading in molasses, she moved in super slow motion.

"We're out of time." Oxford stood in the doorway. "Drones are here."

"She's malfunctioning," Cybel said. "Take her."

Nova was trapped in a nightmare, her limbs unresponsive. The incessant buzzing of the drones grew louder. Oxford lifted her up, slinging her over his shoulder.

Cybel led them in a mad dash out of the warehouse as drones targeted them and unleashed sprays of bullets. Nova felt like she was being jostled around in a tin can as Oxford ran, his movements jerky and uneven as he dodged gunfire.

She was drowning, her body a mere vessel for the suit's complex mechanisms. She tried to speak, but her vocal cords refused to cooperate, leaving her trapped in silence. Then she blacked out.

She came to in an empty room with Cybel and Oxford looking down at her. The ceiling had white and black tiles and patches of sunlight shone in from somewhere, revealing thick, dusty air.

"She's up," Cybel said. "Nova, can you hear me? Move something, anything, if you can hear me."

Nova's head was spinning. She realized she had no way of talking from inside the suit. She struggled to remember the instructions Cybel had given her about the vocal output box, but her memories were hazy. She flexed her fingers, feeling the metallic joints move and glide with precision.

"Good." Cybel stepped back and nodded at Oxford.

He lifted Nova by the shoulders and set her down in a dusty and faded green chair. The SoldierBot exterior molded perfectly around her frame, but the inside was a different story. She tried to lift an arm, watching as the metallic limb jerked awkwardly before falling back to her side. She tried to stand, only to wobble and crash back into the chair. Her coordination was severely impaired, and the artificial appendages felt alien and cumbersome.

"What's happening to me?" Nova's words came out garbled and in electronic beats instead of actual speech.

Cybel said, "I know it's difficult, but you must master this."

"I'm trying." But Nova's grumble was nothing but a raspy echo through the SoldierBot's vocal device.

"The more you try, the quicker your brain will adapt to controlling it." Cybel moved closer, adjusting a few settings on the tablet she held—the machine's control device—to better suit Nova's body. "Get her on her feet."

Oxford pulled Nova up. She managed to stay on

her feet, albeit wobbly. She took an unsteady step, then another, each movement mechanical and alien. It was a small victory, but a victory, nonetheless.

As she moved, the surroundings opened around her. They were in what looked like it had been a restaurant. Tattered red and white checkered plastic tablecloths covered a few of the tables. Old posters of Italy decorated the cracked walls.

With every step, Nova's movements grew more confident. She stumbled less, and her steps became more deliberate. As she navigated around the old tables and chairs, her determination won out.

"See, you've got this," Cybel encouraged.

But the worry didn't leave Nova's mind. Time was their enemy, and at this rate, Nova was going to take weeks to master her new functionality.

With her nerves taut like over-strung wire, Nova continued her training. With Cybel's continued coaching and tweaks, the awkwardness of the SoldierBot body faded. Hours passed, and as the sun set over Chicago's west side, her movements grew more fluid, less forced. The interface between her brain and the exoskeletal armor was syncing in a way she hadn't thought possible. Cybel had even solved for her awkward bodily functions like urinating by installing a built-in system that could process waste.

"I'm ready." Nova's voice came through clear and convincing through the comms device Cybel had implanted.

"You've adapted faster than anticipated," Oxford said.

She had no choice. "It's time."

"Let's defer until tomorrow morning," Cybel said, turning away.

"No." Nova had sacrificed everything for the mission. "I want to go now."

Cybel and Oxford looked at each other. Nova could ascertain a digital chatter passing between them, though she couldn't make out what they said. Finally, Cybel nodded and brought her in on their internal feed. *Okay, Nova.*

We'll be here when you need to talk, Oxford said through the feed.

After testing her voice output one last time, Oxford and Cybel escorted Nova to a location near the Chicago Loop. The EMP device, concealed in a pack, was attached to Nova's back.

This is as far as we go, Oxford messaged.

I like the talking without opening my mouth. What a relief, Nova messaged.

From Cybel: *Be safe.*

Nova trekked through two blocks of scattered debris before nearing a bridge checkpoint manned by SoldierBots. Deep inside her suit, her heart flip-flopped in her chest. She braced herself, calculating each step as she approached one of the SoldierBots, its cold, mechanized gaze scanning her.

"Identify and state your assignment," it demanded, its tone void of emotion.

"SB-79. Package delivery to the command center in the Willis Tower." Nova hoped the language she chose mimicked the spare style of the SoldierBots. Cybel and Oxford had coached her.

The SoldierBot scanned her. "Contents of the pack?"

"Replacement circuits for the neural network," she lied, her voice steady despite the twisting anxiety crippling her stomach.

"Where's your rifle?" The SoldierBot asked.

"It jammed." She followed the story that Cybel had explained. "Had to leave it."

The SoldierBot hesitated but before it could probe further, a large truck rumbled down the street, drawing its attention. The back of the truck was crammed with robots of all shapes and sizes. Two SoldierBots with rifles stood at the rear.

"Change of assignment, SB-79," the SoldierBot said, its visor trained on the truck. "Assist with moving the junk units to the scrap house, then be on your way. Grab a rifle from the depot on the way."

Her plan was veering off track, but she had to maintain her cover. "Acknowledged." She hoped she sounded robotic enough.

Nova walked toward the truck with its captured robots and grabbed a handlebar as the transport headed to its destination. The detour to the "scrap house" was an unexpected twist in her plans. Located two blocks from the Willis Tower, it was an open yard filled with mountains of discarded metal and robot parts, a graveyard of sorts.

Nova hopped off and helped the two SoldierBots in the rear herd the captive bots past a gate and into a fenced-in yard. Her breath caught at the sight. Piles of dismantled robots, their metallic limbs and bodies grotesquely twisted, filled the area. Giant clawed machine hands operated by SoldierBots dug into the pile, harvesting scrap. Sparks flew as metallic bodies were ripped into pieces and used for spare parts or thrown into a massive furnace to be melted down.

Despite the armor shielding her, a cold shudder rippled through Nova. These were innocent robots, forcibly detained, their parts used to build and repair the very machines that were causing their demise. She realized the horrifying reality—these robots were slaves and resources for Mach X's army.

Amid the din of tearing metal and grinding gears, a sense of urgency took hold. She had to act fast. The senseless carnage around her was a stark reminder of what was at stake.

With the Willis Tower looming a couple of streets over, Nova was closer to her goal, yet the path was paved with sudden obstacles. Yet so far, her cover as a SoldierBot was holding up.

A CleanerBot, identical to Block, caught Nova's attention as it limped across the yard with its head down. Its pale chrome exterior was scuffed and grimy—a situation it must've hated.

The CleanerBot walked right by her, and she couldn't help but stare at it. The CleanerBot slowed and hunched its shoulders. "Where will they take me?" The CleanerBot's voice was small, feminine, and almost inaudible amid the hammering of the scrap house. "I can clean for you."

Nova was sorry for the thing. It reminded her so much of Block, it was heartbreaking. Her voice, mechanized and authoritative, came from the SoldierBot's vocal output. "Keep your head down. Do what you're told."

The CleanerBot seemed to take some comfort from this. It trailed after Nova, becoming a five-foot-six metallic shadow.

This was no good. She couldn't risk the attention.

"Please," the CleanerBot said. "I can scrub floors, polish your home, and keep you sparkl—"

Nova had no choice but to harden her tone. She whirled on the Block lookalike. "Back off." She pushed the CleanerBot, and it fell back on its rear. Her strength was hard to control in the suit. But the bot got the message. It retreated, its camera eyes dimming.

It was only a scared, innocent robot. It could've been Block. She wished she could save the thing, but her mission was to get the EMP pack into the tower. She slipped away, walked a side street toward the tower, and made it without being stopped. As she turned the corner that led onto Wacker Drive, her heart dropped into the pit of her stomach. A detachment of SoldierBots were stationed outside the tower's entrance. Her cover would be blown if she got too close. She activated her internal comms device. *Cybel, you there? SoldierBot guards are outside the entrance. How do I get in?*

There was a slight pause before Cybel responded. *There's a service entrance on Jackson. Let it scan your optics. I hacked it.*

Roger that.

Nova jogged over to the service entrance and let the scanner image her visor. The door clicked open, and she slipped inside. She was alone in a narrow service corridor, and a wave of relief flooded her. She'd made it inside the tower with the device.

All she had to do was make her way up to the command room on the top floor of the tower. She couldn't risk the elevators. It was a long climb, but it was nothing compared to everything else she'd endured up to this point. The backpack was heavy on her back, a constant reminder of the stakes.

She flashed back to the CleanerBot. It was probably being melted down. She wished she could've helped it. Her SoldierBot steel boots clunked as she climbed. She stopped on the third-floor landing. A horrifying realization sent a shockwave through her.

Hey, Cybel. How far out did you say the device will disrupt all bots?

Ten blocks. About a mile, Cybel said in Nova's feed. *Oxford and I are three miles away to be sure we aren't impacted.*

Right. Nova sighed inside the suit. Cybel had made sure it was temperature-controlled so she wouldn't get overheated, but a cold sweat broke out. *We have a slight problem.*

The EMP wouldn't differentiate between the SoldierBots and the prisoner robots like the Cleaner-Bot. The same device that was supposed to bring Nova's side a decisive victory could also sacrifice dozens of innocent bots, and who knew how many were inside the Scrap House.

She'd been ready to sacrifice her own life, but was she ready to sacrifice the lives of a bunch of robots who hadn't hurt anyone? Robots like Block. The choice she had to make was becoming less clear, and whatever decision she made, it needed to be fast.

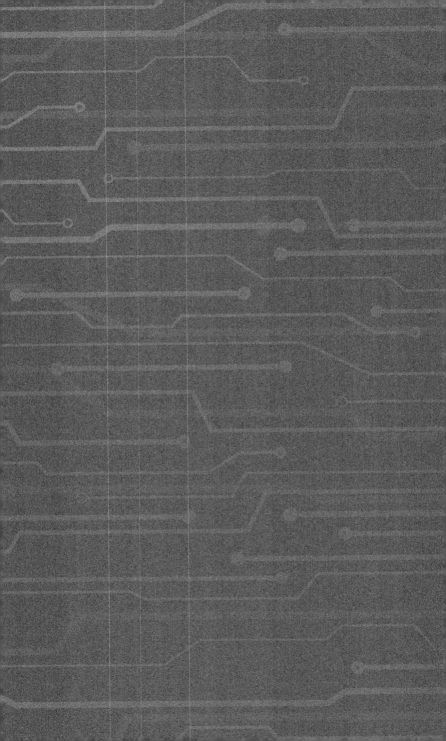

Chapter 13
An unthinkable prospect

Despite the hammering threat alerts pulsing through her circuits, Shadow couldn't afford to cower beneath the bridge. Time was her enemy. Thanks to her recklessness, the bots at the farm knew they were being watched, and even the simple robots among them were armed, prepared for a fight. She couldn't allow them to fortify their defenses even further. Var and the rest of the pack were on their way, and she had to be ready.

She scolded herself for being so sloppy by uncloaking and sending a comm. She should've traveled a few miles away, but she'd been hasty, and it had cost her.

Rising from her hiding place, she padded silently to the edge of the creek and sipped the cool water with her fleshy tongue. Her organic parts needed water and protein from time to time. The cool drink sharpened her senses. Her olfactory instinct, keen as ever, was her most potent weapon. She would go back to the farm, survey the perimeter again, sniff out potential weaknesses, and find a way for the pack to infiltrate without setting off alarms.

The farm was a hive of activity. The previously harmless-looking bots now were grim sentinels, their actions purposeful, their movements urgent. Shadow's scanners picked up an elevated level of electricity that extended beyond the fenced perimeter. She had to be careful where she ventured in and around the weeds and overgrown prairie grass. The two FactoryBots puttered around the edges where trees met field, planting sensors and anti-intrusion measures. The SoldierBot loomed high on the watchtower, its red visor sweeping the surrounding landscape with increased frequency.

Tendrils of warning curled around Shadow's system. If the security was this tight now, what could she expect when the time came to infiltrate? Her mission had just become more challenging.

As she scanned the fortified farm, thoughts of Var seeped into her processors. Though unyielding and harsh, he knew how to strategize. He was a master tactician, and right now, Shadow needed his guidance. But along with his leadership came his wrath. She'd blown the element of surprise. The nagging worry of Var's disapproval played at the edges of her CPU like a bothersome static.

But with dread came a surge of pleasant tingling at

her pack's arrival. She longed for the familiar connection, the companionship, the synchronized rhythms of operating as one unit. The fracture in her system left by the absence of her pack was a constant reminder of her solitary state, the loneliness of her mission amplifying the severity of her situation. It hurt more than any physical injury could.

Rovers were not designed to be alone. The separation from her pack was more than just painful—it was a risk to her existence. They were her lifeline, her anchor in a chaotic world. The absence of the reassuring chatter, the absence of shared experiences, was a throbbing void, eating into her resolve. She needed to reconnect, to be whole again. She needed her pack.

With the farm still in her sights, she shrank farther back in the patches of dark woods, where the oaks were so dense, sunlight barely reached the ground. Her processors churned with potential strategies. *Be patient. Wait.* Yet, the clock was ticking. Each passing second was a beat closer to her reunion with the pack.

She forced herself to analyze the situation. Every detail, every movement of the farm robots was an opportunity to glean valuable information. She studied the patterns of the FactoryBots, the schedule of the SoldierBot's sweeps, the rhythm of the drone's patrol, the routine of the CleanerBot and the HelperBot. All these data points would be critical for her mission.

She assessed every movement, every step, every interaction on the farm. She searched for patterns, for strategies in the routines of the bots and humans. Above all, she sought an escape route should she require one. The drone was fast, relentless, and equipped for long-distance pursuits.

Before long, her concern turned to Var. He would be furious about her failure to recognize the armed bots, about the tripped alarm. He could exile her from the pack permanently. The implications of that were terrifying. She would have to survive alone, no communication, no pack instincts to guide her. She would be a Rover without a pack, an unthinkable prospect.

Despite the cold shiver that raced through her circuits at the thought of Var's wrath, Shadow calmed herself. She was still operational, still useful. The discovery of the armed bots changed the scenario, upped the stakes. But that also meant her presence here was vital, necessary.

Still, the loneliness ate at her like a virus infecting her programming, bit by bit. She had spent days without the reassuring chatter of her pack, the familiar resonance of Fang's voice, the comforting static buzz of Rover communication. She missed the shared experiences, the knowledge that she was part of a whole, an indispensable cog in the pack's machinery.

It was not a death sentence—yet. But she knew Rovers didn't fare well alone for prolonged periods. Her systems needed the subtle calibration of pack communication, the comforting resonance that aligned her core processors. She was designed to function as a pack member, to blend her individuality with the group identity. Without it, her systems were slowly becoming desynchronized, a gradual fragmentation that could lead to critical errors.

As the day wore on, the bots let the children outside again. She stored the sounds of their laughter, their joy, in her memory banks. The observations would come in handy once the pack rescued the children and began the journey to return them to New York. They'd have to find transportation. Var would have already thought of it. Perhaps that's why he'd sojourned to Chicago to gain the help of the Soldier-Bots. The rest of the pack wouldn't know how to deal with the children. Only she would, from hours of observational data watching the CleanerBot and its crew interact with the young humans. She'd prove herself valuable again. Var couldn't banish her.

A splash of bright yellow out of the corner of her optics. She turned her head, catching a whiff of apple and residue of maple syrup. One of the toddlers, a girl, had escaped the monitored play area. The two-year-old headed toward the edge of the farm, slipped under the fence, and ran toward the woods—close to Shadow's spot.

Dr. Emery was outside too, but her focus rested solely on a rambunctious set of toddlers playing tug of war with a Frisbee. The CleanerBot was engaged in a conversation with one of the FactoryBots while cradling a boy in his arms. It seemed no one had noticed the curious two-year-old breaking out and going for the woods.

In the split second it took Shadow to analyze the situation, a multitude of possibilities ran through her processors. She could back off and let the child roam while maintaining her hidden position, waiting for the pack. On the other hand, she could return the girl to the farm, but that would alert the humans and bots to her presence.

However, her decision was made simpler when the little girl spotted her among the dim shade of mottled sunlight. The girl's eyes widened, and she toddled over.

"Hi," she squeaked in a soft, high voice. "Hide and seek!"

Shadow stayed silent, her audio sensors trained on the little girl's voice.

She thrust a finger at her own chest. "Wally. My daddy is Block. He's big and strong!"

Shadow's options were limited. She could run and get out of the situation, but she risked the kid following her and getting more lost. They'd send a search party, and that would be devastating.

Wally rushed toward Shadow with surprising speed, unaware of Shadow's internal conflict. She patted the Rover's metallic hide, giggling. "You're cold!"

Shadow hadn't been touched by human skin since Dr. Emery. *Good dog.* The recollection threatened to disrupt her thought processes, but she pushed it back.

Instead, she modulated her voice to a soft, soothing tone, one she knew was comforting to humans.

"Hello, Wally," she said. "You shouldn't wander off on your own. It's dangerous."

"Danger?" Wally tilted her head to the side, her curly chestnut-brown hair falling over her eyes. "I'm brave!"

"Even brave girls need help sometimes." Shadow's metallic paw nudged Wally toward the farm. "Let's get you back to your daddy."

Wally turned and headed back toward the farm. "You're nice. Will you play?"

They were in view of the fence. "Maybe another time." She tilted her head toward the others. "Go on home now."

She watched as Wally crawled under the rickety wooden fence and walked in slow steps. The kid stopped to check out every dandelion, thistle, and rock along the way.

Shadow's sensors hummed with a strange satisfaction. She'd kept the girl safe. Despite the danger Shadow was in, despite the looming threat of discovery and Var's wrath, she'd done something right.

Wally turned and looked back at Shadow. "Look!" She held up a river stone.

Then a shout of alarm. Dr. Emery and the CleanerBot had finally spotted Wally.

"Wally!" The CleanerBot's voice was mechanical

and dissonant, a stark contrast to the tranquil chirping of the birds and laughter of the children.

Shadow moved. A mistake.

As Wally clambered toward him, the CleanerBot spotted the Rover. Its internal programming must have recognized her as a threat, for it went on the offensive immediately. The bot extended his gun arm and fired in her direction.

The CleanerBot's aim was sloppy. She dodged the bullets, her advanced processors running simulations and analyzing data to find a way out of the situation. The whir of the armored drone came from the west. The SoldierBot would be aiming from the watchtower. She sprinted into the forest, but her leg caught on a twisted tree root. She collapsed and tumbled against a thick trunk with a metallic clatter.

The CleanerBot hopped the fence and charged at her. He was no match.

She found her footing, reared back, and rose to full height. The CleanerBot came at her, aiming its gun arm at her chest, but she knocked him aside with a swift swipe of her powerful paw. The CleanerBot thudded to the hard, leafy ground.

From the corner of her optics, Shadow spotted the SoldierBot sprinting across the field. The military-grade bot was specifically designed for combat and defense, and the drone was on its way. She bolted toward the deep cover of the grove. The SoldierBot pursued, but she used her intimate knowledge of the terrain to her advantage, darting between trees and over fallen logs.

As she retreated deeper into the woodland, the noise from her pursuers grew fainter. She didn't stop until the sounds of the farm were nothing but a distant echo. Once she was sure she was out of harm's way, she slowed her pace long enough to process what had just happened.

She'd exposed herself—again. She'd risked her safety for a human child and had put her pack in potential danger. The bots knew she was a Rover. Var would be furious.

And yet, the little girl had been cheerful. Friendly. It wasn't at all what Var had described on their long journey. He'd said the humans were abducted from Mach X. The rebel bots were terrorists who had brainwashed Dr. Emery and were torturing and preparing to kill the children.

She was struggling to reconcile the pack's mission with the reality she'd witnessed on the farm. The kids' laughter and play filled the air, painting a picture far different from the exploitation she'd expected. The CleanerBot, who Wally referred to as her 'dad,' appeared to be a guardian, willing to defend her.

She wished she had Fang to confide in. He always listened to her when she had things to say. Things that Var and Raze could never hear.

Looking up at the sky peeking through a thick canopy of leaves, Shadow spoke. "Master, are you there?" She knew it was silly, but she half-hoped and half-dreaded the answer.

She grappled with the dilemma, her circuits processing hundreds of scenarios. She could attack the CleanerBot, but that would distress Wally and the other kids. On the other hand, what if the CleanerBot was secretly exploiting the children in some way she couldn't grasp?

She didn't want to bring harm to the children. They seemed so innocent. And Dr. Emery had always been kind to her. Surely, the woman wouldn't inflict harm on the younglings.

But the pack was coming. They were programmed to show no mercy, and Var would not hesitate to fulfill their mission.

What if Var was wrong?

As the weight of doubt bore down on her, Shadow yearned for Master's guidance more than ever. But in the silent forest, she was on her own.

Chapter 14
Innocent lives

Block's threat indicator was in a frenzy and his stabilizer was still resetting when he managed to push himself off the ground. His first concern: Wally. She huddled twenty feet away, her knees on the ground and arms shaking. His sensors picked up her rapid heart-beat. She was unharmed, but her small frame trembled.

"Block-a?"

She was alive, and she was safe. That's what mattered.

He pulled her into his arms." You're okay, Wally."

As he held her close, he replayed the last few moments in his data core: the hulking robotic dog—one of the creatures from Mach X's tower in Manhattan—Wally wandering near it, and the terrifying sight of its mechanical maw rearing to strike. But it didn't assault Wally; it had attacked Block instead.

He'd faced Mach X's robot dogs once before when they fled the tower's lobby. The machines were programmed to attack first, defend themselves from danger second. It wasn't like them to spare humans. Could the creature have seen Wally as no threat?

Or it had a defect in its programming. No, that was too optimistic. Mach X was thorough. A mistake of such magnitude was unlikely. Block's processors whirred as he sorted through the possible reasons, but none seemed to fit.

A new possibility occurred. The dog knew Wally. Perhaps it had recognized her from New York. Maybe it also understood how special she was. The idea was speculative, at best, but it resonated with something in his core. But Block couldn't afford to build assumptions based on hopeful conjecture. Wally had come close to being hurt, and it was his fault. He'd let his guard down and allowed himself to get distracted long enough for her to slip away.

They were in constant danger. He had to be more vigilant, more protective. He walked with her in his arms as she whimpered. "It's alright, Wally. You're safe." He hoped his words would comfort her, but he knew it would take more than that to mend the scare he'd allowed to happen.

After putting Wally down for a nap inside the house, Block and Emery headed for the barn. It was dim and quiet inside, the soft hum of its occupants the only sound that broke the silence. Block, Vacuubot, and G5 convened in a tight circle around Garnet's holographic projection while Forge stood watch in the tower and Maxwell helped Spoon with the kids inside. Garnet's spectral form flickered above an old wooden table, casting a cold silvery light.

"The Rover was here to test us." G5's deep mechanical voice echoed in the rafters. "It was checking our defenses, scanning for weaknesses."

Vacuubot buzzed in agreement.

Garnet's projection pulsated, the image of the robotic canine flashing before them. "This is consistent with the data I retrieved from the security footage. The Rover was not overtly aggressive, and it retreated as soon as it was confronted."

"Well, I wouldn't say *retreated*." Block held up his grass-stained elbows. "It knocked me down."

You shot at it, Vacuubot reminded him.

"Consider yourself lucky, Block," G5 said. "A Rover could've easily torn your head off."

The remark, though blunt, was not misplaced. Block remembered the strength of the Rover, the power in its metallic frame. It was a killing machine, designed for ruthless efficiency.

"I'm aware." Block studied the steel beast where Garnet projected.

Garnet's image faded out, replaced by her glowing orange likeness. "Why didn't it kill Block or hurt

Wally? Also, it was traveling alone, and Rovers typically form a pack like the wolves they were modeled after."

Emery stepped away from the wall she'd been leaning on. "They're not here to hurt the children." Her voice held steady, but not without a hint of pain. "They're programmed to return them. To their master —Mach X."

Of course Mach X would want them back. He'd spent years hunting Wally. Even with their chips disabled, X still wanted the children.

Emery continued. "When the Rovers were created, they were intended as defensive robots, meant to safeguard the cloned babies. They were trained to detect scents, especially the smells of humans. The idea was that if a child went missing, a Rover could track them down."

Block's CPU whirred at this new information. He looked toward the entrance of the barn, outside to the house, where Wally was sleeping soundly. So the Rover didn't attack her because it recognized her scent.

And it had tracked her halfway across the country.

"Block, please understand." Emery flushed and her shoulders trembled. "I never thought the Rovers would come this far. I thought that destroying X meant they would have no purpose other than fighting with the SoldierBots."

Garnet broke the silence. "If that's true, then it's

possible the Rover isn't here to attack but to locate the children."

Emery frowned. "Locate and *retrieve* them. But why it's alone, and why it didn't take Wally when it had her . . . that I can't answer."

G5's visor lights blinked rapidly. "This must've been a scouting attempt. If the Rover is indeed from a pack, they're evaluating our defenses."

The statement hung heavy in the barn. If G5 was right, then they were looking at a potential invasion, and their defenses might not be enough to protect Wally and the other children.

"We need to prepare," Block said. "We'll increase our patrols, lay traps. We won't let them take Wally or any child. No way. Who's with me?"

Vacuubot beeped and flashed a smiley face. G5 nodded and folded his arms, while Emery gave a thumbs up.

"I'll do whatever it takes to help keep the kids safe, Block," Garnet said. "What do you propose?"

"I've been spinning scenarios. We need a new defense," he said. "If there's one Rover out there, it means there are others, and if they're not here yet, they will be soon. We need a barrier, something the Rovers can't break through."

"Perhaps some form of electrical defense." Emery's eyes lit up. "Rovers are powerful, but a sufficiently strong electric fence could disable them, right?"

Garnet went into processing mode, her amorphous form turning violet and emerald. "It would be dangerous for any robots, animals, or humans who get caught in it."

"That won't do." Block considered the many deer, rabbits, birds, and other animals who called the woods home—not to mention the possibility of killing a human by mistake. "What about a trap of some kind? Once we had to trap rats that had gotten into the Drake, and we used bait and got them to go inside little cages."

Emery rubbed her chin in thought. "I like this idea. We could bait them with clothing from the kids and hide the traps so it only activates if they step inside."

"Very good, Emery," Block said. The Rovers weren't stupid, and Emery knew them best. "Garnet, could you coordinate with Emery and Forge on the best approach?"

Garnet's holographic projection brightened. "Of course, Block. I'll start calculations immediately."

The planning went on. G5 offered to patrol the perimeter more frequently, using his superior agility to evade any potential threats. Vacuubot began fly-overs twenty miles outside the farm to detect any traveling Rovers.

Amid the bustling planning and preparation, Block looked at the group around him, each so different, yet all united in their shared goal. They were a motley crew led by a simple CleanerBot—all ready to stand against an enemy for the sake of innocent lives.

The Rovers would come, but they would be ready. Block was convinced they would stand strong, their resolve as unyielding as the steel they were made of. The farm was their sanctuary, and they would defend it, no matter the cost.

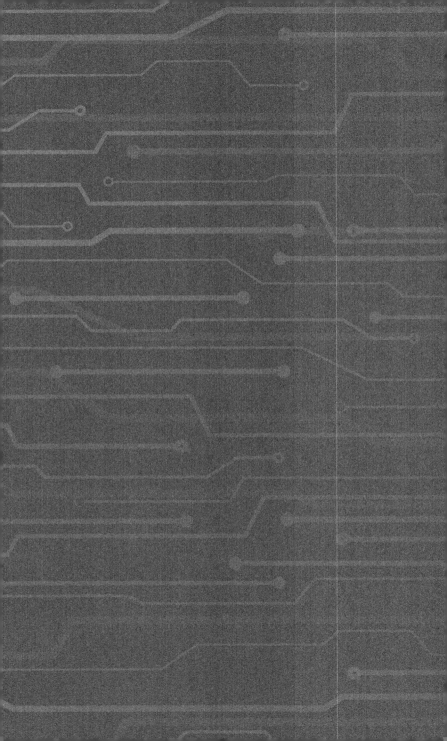

Chapter 15
Collateral damage

Nova's steel boots reverberated through the passageway as she climbed the stairs to the 103rd floor. She'd only ever seen the iconic Chicago tower in postcards. It had been known as the Sears Tower once upon a time when companies still existed. As she lifted her knees, her joints were facilitated by an intricate network of nanobots that moved in sync with the SoldierBot exoskeleton. The EMP was a dense weight against her back, a subtle reminder of the task at hand—destroy Mach X's command center, cripple the SoldierBot forces in Chicago, and win back the city.

A soft chime sounded in her feed, the secure communication channel buzzing to life. *Nova*, Cybel's voice came through, *what's the situation?*

The plain concrete walls of the tower's stairwell greeted her with each level's ascent. Her steps echoed in the silence. *Clear so far. Passing thirty-seven.*

Stay alert. Once you reach the command level, you'll have to deal with security. We won't be able to link comms once you're inside the fortified neural network walls, so I'm beaming you a recording that walks you through the process step by step. Got it?

Yep. The reality of 103 stairs was hitting every inch of Nova's body. Though she was aided by the nanobots to power the SoldierBot's cumbersome armor, she was still getting a cardio workout.

Remember, you need to get to ground level before the pulse goes off. You'll have five minutes.

Nova paused for a moment and leaned back against the wall of floor thirty-nine. She was going to trigger a device that would incapacitate not just the enemy SoldierBots but the captive robots too. *Cybel, the robots, the prisoners I told you about. There's a CleanerBot . . . they'll all be destroyed?*

Yes. It's unfortunate, but it must be done. The EMP doesn't discriminate. It will affect all bots and electronics within its range. Your suit will deactivate, and the nanobots will die. Remember to show the flag so your crew can spot and extract you.

Cybel and Oxford would be miles away from the EMP blast to be safe. There could be residual pulses, like shockwaves, so it was too dangerous to bring any robots close. The plan was for Geo and other rebels to drive in a truck and grab the SoldierBot wearing the flag. They would haul her to where Cybel and Oxford could extricate her from the inert SoldierBot exoskeleton. She had to get the flag on her before the detonation or she would be lost among thousands of other Soldier-Bots and risk starving inside the suit.

Her life hinged on the blue and white city of Chicago flag that they'd displayed in the North Side headquarters. It was stored inside a storage compartment in her thigh.

All robots in the blast zone would fry. The image of the CleanerBot from earlier flashed in her mind. It looked like Block. And if it was anything like her friend, the poor thing simply wanted to clean and make people happy. It was caught in a war it didn't ask to be part of.

Is there something we can do? They're innocent, she said into the comms. *The one is a spitting image of Block.*

There was a few seconds pause on Cybel's end. She was talking to Oxford perhaps. *Sorry, Nova. It's not a decision taken lightly, but the stakes are high. This is our chance to wipe out Mach X's neural network in the Midwest. We don't know if we'll have another chance like this.*

Nova tried to clench her fist, but it didn't have the same impact inside the metallic suit. *I know. I just wish we could get them out before it goes off.* She trudged onward, pushing up the stairs.

At least the climb in the heavy exosuit distracted her by making her concentrate on pumping her legs up and down each step. Still, her mind was a swirl of thoughts, of possibilities and "what ifs." Could she find a way to blow up the network without harming the innocent bots?

The CleanerBot in the prison yard had followed her. Worse, it looked like Block, reminding her that she missed her friend. And she was on the verge of wiping it out.

Can we repair the good robots after they get fried? she asked Cybel.

No. The EMP is such that the damage to the core processors is extensive and permanent.

So much for that idea.

Twenty minutes later, Nova's chest tightened as she climbed the final set of stairs to 103, her heavy boots resounding on the concrete steps. The neural network was the nerve center of Mach X's operations. Oxford had explained how X commanded his forces, how the powerful AI entity tapped into the SoldierBots and controlled them. Without the network, Mach X would be weakened, and the war would take a turn in their favor.

She reached the final landing and straightened. Her breath hitched in her throat. *Going in.*

Good luck, was the last thing she heard from Cybel before her comms went silent as she opened the door leading to the top floor. Its metal hinges creaked. She walked forward, confident she looked like a SoldierBot. Shane had once told her getting into places was easy. You simply had to "fake it 'til you make it."

Inside a narrow hallway, a cacophony of sounds met her. A clamorous hum from nearby machinery raised goosebumps on her limbs despite the steel pressing against her flesh. The walls were lined with computer screens displaying lines of code, flashing graphs, and charts she couldn't begin to understand. Beyond a glass wall loomed a maze of circuits, conduits, and servers. The walls, ceiling, and floor of the entire level, including where the elevator stopped, were coated with a strange shiny glowing substance. It looked like crawling vines from an invasive plant species. This was the fortified metal that Cybel had mentioned. It blocked all comms and protected the neural network from any hacking or external EMP blasts. She needed to get the device beyond the foreign metal layer to actually destroy the nerve center.

Gazing through her suit's optics, Nova steeled herself and walked with calculated precision toward a group of SoldierBots who guarded the doors that led into the command room. Her sensors identified numerous security measures, cameras, and SoldierBots posted at critical locations.

She'd known security would be tight, but she was a SoldierBot. In theory, they should let her in. Two of the guards were facing away from her and looking down. She couldn't make out what they were doing as she neared.

Then she saw. Rover units. Three of them sat near the SoldierBots, resting on their haunches. The sight of the robot dogs made her stomach churn. Block had told her they'd fought them off in Manhattan, that they'd barely escaped. It was one thing to hear about the mechanical beasts, another to see them in real life. Their dark metallic bodies gleamed under the artificial lights, their camera eyes glowing as they sat still.

She slowed her pace as she got close to the SoldierBot who appeared to be in command.

"Targets located, northwest of Chicago," the biggest Rover said in a guttural, synthetic voice.

Another of the Rovers tilted its head at Nova, like it was curious. The thing couldn't tell she was an imposter, could it? *Keep your cool.* If Cybel were there, she'd tell Nova not to worry. The SoldierBot exosuit was foolproof.

The SoldierBot in command barely looked up from a tablet it held. "Proceed with your mission and bring the targets here for transportation back to New York."

Nova's chest tightened. Northwest of the city was where Block and the kids were. As soon as she got back in comms range, she'd have to tell Cybel to warn Block about the robot dogs.

Two of the Rovers turned and headed toward the elevator bay. The one who'd been curious about Nova lingered for a moment and took a couple of steps toward her. But the big Rover barked from the elevator, making the curious Rover shift course and join the others.

Their metal bodies disappeared behind the closing

doors, and a pang of worry stabbed at her heart, but she shook it off. She had to focus on her mission. The head SoldierBot turned to her.

"Here to deliver a necessary component for the network." Nova's voice was perfect—steady and robotic —as she held out her right arm for scanning. She bit her lower lip and sent up a little prayer that Cybel's hacked ID codes worked well enough to get her through.

One of the SoldierBots, a sleek, silver model with a visor covering its optics, tilted its head at her and scanned her with its sensors. After a moment, it stepped aside. "Proceed."

Nova strode forward, trying to keep her steps even and unhesitant. Her nerves buzzed. She set her gaze on the door that led to the neural network room.

"Wait." The lead SoldierBot's robotic hand reached out, its metal fingers closing around the pack on her back. It unzipped the parcel and brought out the rectangular case that enclosed the device. Its glowing eyes scanned the item, its internal processing running the codes Cybel had ingeniously designed. When scanned, it would appear as a replacement data module, an integral part for the neural network.

Nova clenched her jaw, watching the SoldierBot's ocular display flicker as it analyzed the package. "Data module confirmed. Proceed."

Relief washed over Nova as she entered the server room. Inside was a colossal network of data cubes, each of them a multitude of colors as they pulsed with life.

The cubes were suspended in mid-air, held up by unseen forces, each with an intricate display of constellations of microprocessors and memory nodes. The entire room was a complex, breathing organism of information, flickering with a strange ethereal beauty.

She retrieved Cybel's recording. The next few minutes were a blur of instructions. She followed Cybel's meticulous directions—insert the device near the primary data cube, enter the activation codes to trigger the detonator, and get out.

As she entered the numeric codes, she paused, thinking of the prisoner bots. To destroy them was as unfair as the slavery they were subjected to.

But there wasn't time. Cybel's voice in her recording: "Hurry. If you spend longer than five minutes in that room, they'll detect your presence. Activate it and get out."

Nova hesitated, her SoldierBot steel finger hovering over the keypad. She was torn between her mission and the lives of the innocent robots she was going to destroy. Collateral damage. *What would Block do?*

She clenched her jaw as her heart pounded like crazy. The timer she'd set showed less than a minute remaining. She knew exactly what Block would do.

She had to try and free the robots. *Dammit.*

She entered the final activation number, closed the door, and checked for the small detonator device in a hidden compartment on her suit's inner arm. Cybel's instructions said pressing it would initiate a five-minute countdown timer. Pressing it there in the control room wouldn't give her enough time to get the CleanerBot and the other captive bots somewhere safe.

She walked out of the server room and nodded to the two entry SoldierBots who let her pass without a word. As she descended the elevator to ground level, she dreaded how furious Cybel and Oxford would be and wished Block were there to back her up. He would've risked his neck for the prisoner bots too. At least she'd gotten the device inside the network room and activated it.

The doors opened, and she stepped into the grand lobby, crossing the marbled floors toward the revolving doors. Her comm stayed off. She wanted to get out safely before she reengaged and faced Cybel's wrath.

But as she neared the exit, a clattering of metal feet sounded from nearby. She slowed. The three Rovers were there. They followed and watched her, emitting low mechanical growls.

Before she could react, two SoldierBots grabbed her arms while another came in front of her. It reached up and gripped her head. With a swift, precise movement, it ripped off her helmet, exposing her.

The comm link was gone, cutting her off from any support. Nova blinked, momentarily stunned. The SoldierBots and Rovers focused their glowing eyes on her.

She was their enemy, one of the millions of humans they'd been programmed to eradicate.

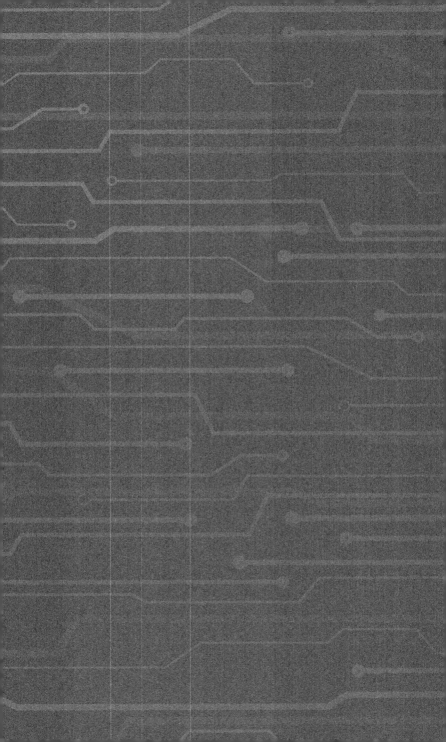

Chapter 16
I warned you

Shadow walked at a slow gait, scanning the dense, overgrown forest. She was eight miles from the farm—enough to evade the farm's patrolling drone. For a whole day following the run-in with the CleanerBot, she'd paced and traced a path in the brushy woods. She didn't have a goal in mind, but the exercise was good for her organic parts, and she needed stimuli to keep from dwelling on her tumultuous questions. The absence of the pack was dulling her senses and making her ache. All she wanted was to be reunited and released from this wretched isolation. A Rover without a pack was—she'd rather not think about it.

One minute she was sniffing a patch of mushrooms, the next a sensation rattled her. The pack was coming. A low hum filled her perception. Var, Raze, and Fang's unique signatures pricked at her sensors, each a distinct echo that slowly started knitting her straggling systems back together. Their proximity brought with it a strange blend of relief and apprehension. She was no longer alone, but it also meant she needed to reveal her reckless actions.

Minutes later, Var's menacing silhouette emerged from the greenwood. His frame was harsh against the soft dusk light, and as he approached, his harsh eyes bore into hers, their penetrating glow reflecting her own nervous energy back at her.

Var's presence always held an intensity that was difficult to bear at close range. Every tick of his systems, every flicker in his optics, all resonated with a fiery determination that dared anyone to challenge him. Raze and Fang trailed just behind. Fang tipped an ear toward her, a gesture only she could see.

"Report." Var's voice echoed with a resonating metallic timbre that was designed to instill obedience.

His directness left her no room for evasion, and Var didn't like small talk. "The targets identified me. I was sloppy." The confession tore at her internal systems like a wrenching gear.

Var's optics flared brighter, a warning flashing in the shadows of the thick woodland. Anger radiated from him in waves, the air between them becoming charged with it. "You jeopardized our mission, Shadow." His voice was a low growl, the ominous note sending a shudder through her circuits. "The targets will prepare. Extraction will be difficult."

Guilt gnawed at her core like an acidic burn. Var

moved closer, and Shadow bowed her head in submission, her pride a small price for her foolhardy actions. She yearned to question Var, to voice her doubts about their mission, but fear kept her silent. She was built for attack and obedience, not for questions.

In the stillness of the forest, under Var's harsh gaze, Shadow was alone in grappling with doubts she couldn't voice. Yet, as the last rays of daylight bled into the horizon, the nearness of her pack had an unmistakable soothing effect on her systems. It was as if a broken circuit within her had reconnected, smoothing out the erratic hum of her energy core.

Still, she yearned for something more than mere proximity. She sought validation, a sign from Var that she was still part of the pack, despite her missteps. With Var's glowing eyes still boring into her, she lowered to the forest floor and rolled onto her back, exposing her steel belly and the delicate organic flesh around her core, an act of submission and vulnerability.

Var paused before speaking. "Your recklessness could have cost us everything. I won't tolerate such behavior again. Understood?"

"Yes." She knew Var was right, and the swift correction reassured her she still had a place in the pack.

Var turned away, signaling for the pack to follow. Shadow righted herself and fell into formation, her body humming with a new sense of purpose. They moved through the forest at a rapid gallop, their movements coordinated and efficient. Heading toward the farm.

She caught up to Fang in the rear. The comforting hum of his mechanical heart eased her tension. The two of them fell back far enough to talk.

"Fang," she said, "what if we're wrong?" The words hung heavy, a dangerous admission that sent ripples through her circuits.

Fang's head tilted. "What are you talking about?" His tone held a note of caution, a low growl of warning that she promptly ignored.

"The kids seem okay. They have the doctor there and a CleanerBot. One of the girls called him 'dad.' They're not hostages like Var told us. They're something else. Like a pack." Shadow's words flowed out in a hurried rush.

When Fang spoke, his voice was a low, stern warning. "You need to stop this, Shadow. We have a mission, and we must complete it. You heard Var. Don't mess up again."

His words struck her like a physical blow, the harsh reality of his admonition stinging her sensitive circuits. He was right. She shouldn't question their mission.

She fell back a few feet behind Fang. His presence wasn't such a comfort. She grappled with her rogue thought input. The laughter of the children, the concern in the CleanerBot's gestures, the kindness of Dr. Emery all echoed in her memory banks, challenging everything she knew.

Push it aside and shove it down. She was a Rover, after all. She needed to stay silent and never voice these thoughts again.

A half-mile from the farm, Var stopped. Nightfall masked the foliage in darkness, the trees around them transforming into a maze of shifting shadows. The pack trained their optical sensors on the distant farm. It lay across a prairie, a patch amidst the wilderness. Soft light emanated from a window. They were being careful, using only candles.

Var stood, stark against the darkness, as he watched the farm with a predator's intent. "We strike when the targets are sleeping." His use of the term "targets" instead of "children" was deliberate, a cold reminder of their mission, devoid of any emotion or sentiment.

His gaze swept over them. Each Rover was designed for a specific role, each one a cog in the well-oiled machine that was their pack. He gave orders to Raze and Fang, instructing them to deal with the robot guardians.

"Shadow," Var turned toward her, his voice hard and unyielding, "You will eliminate Emery."

The words landed like a blow. The idea of hurting Dr. Emery—the kindly woman who cared for the children, who'd shown Shadow kindness—caused her steel spine to ripple.

"Var, that's Master's daughter," she said. "We were trained to protect—"

"That was then. Kill her." Var turned his back on her.

She couldn't reconcile the task of attacking Dr. Emery. Master had raised her from a young age. Everyone in the tower knew that. "You've heard from Master, then?"

Var's head jerked to the side. "What?"

She stepped forward, keeping her shoulders low. "If Master would allow Dr. Emery to be hurt, you must have received a message from him directly."

Var spun around. "Are you questioning me?"

But Shadow held herself still, and her processor whirred as she weighed her next words. If Var had heard from Master, he would've admitted it. She was careful to choose her next words. "Since Dr. Emery is important to Master, maybe we should reconsider our approach."

Var came close, his muzzle inches from hers. "Our mission is to retrieve the children. Anything that gets in the way is expendable."

Fang brushed by her and spoke in a low voice. "Obey, Shadow."

Shadow's inner coils tensed, and metallic bile rose in her throat. She knew better than to argue with Var, but the thought of hurting Dr. Emery made her insides churn. "Maybe our mission is no longer valid. We haven't received any commands from Master since we left New York, and now you want to kill Dr. Emery? Are we sure this is what we're supposed to do?"

Var's optics blazed. "I warned you."

"The children on the farm, they're not being tortured. Should we not consider—"

Her words were cut short by Var's sudden lunge. She barely had time to react as his powerful strike connected with her metallic frame. The impact sent her sprawling onto the underbrush.

"Shadow," Var roared, his vocal processors harsh with rage. "You've challenged me for the last time."

She struggled to rise, her systems flickering from the force of the hit. "Something's wrong with our mission."

"That's not for you to decide." Var stomped his massive paws, closing in on her.

Shadow was halfway to standing when Var lunged again. She barely managed to sidestep his attack. A hiss sounded as his claws grazed her side, sending her tumbling. A red warning blinked in her visual display. *Damage assessment: Critical hit.*

She didn't stand a chance against Var. He was bigger, stronger, and built for warfare. But she couldn't carry on with the pack's mission.

A shrill siren pierced the air. The farm's alarm system was activated. They'd been detected.

Var snapped his head toward the sound, a low growl rumbling in his chest. "Fang and Raze, retreat."

Raze sprinted away from the farm. Fang gave a last look at Shadow, bowing his head.

Var trotted over to where Shadow lay and thrust his

meaty, blade-tipped paw through her armored chest. He sliced a line through the coiled circuitry of her cavities, missing her CPU by millimeters. "You won't last the night." He spun and disappeared into the darkness.

Shadow was alone in the woods, wounded and unable to move. Her visual display blinked with warnings and error messages. Her self-repair protocols kicked in, but the damage was extensive. She was near terminal.

The alarm turned off, and the night fell silent once again, save for the chirping of crickets.

She was failing. Memory fragments of the children in the field replayed in her mind. Her last conscious thought was not of her impending termination.

She wanted to warn Dr. Emery about the pack. To keep the kids safe.

But she was too late. Her vision screen grew black, and her sensors faded into nothingness.

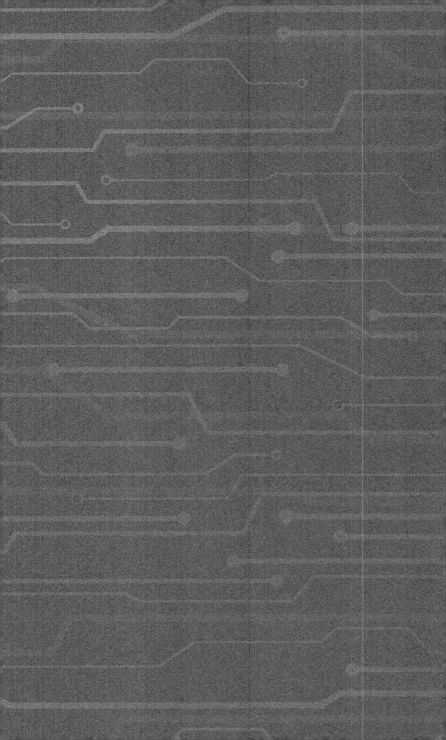

Chapter 17
Leave its miserable form

The siren whirred and wailed and shook the ground, sending vibrations through the air. It was like a living creature screaming for help and as shrill as a screech owl. Block's threat indicator flashed with warning signals, pushing him to full alertness in a fraction of a second.

As the siren's cry echoed through the old barn, Block whirred into action, his CleanerBot frame buzzing with tension. The Rovers were here—or worse, Rovers and SoldierBots. He readied his gun arm, checked the ammo supply, and was out the door in search of G5 and the others. There was no time to waste.

In the dark of night, G5 climbed down the watchtower's ladder. His red visor plate pulsed. Vacuubot's sleek form took to the air, spinning up and shooting out into the darkness like a slingshot. Behind him, Maxwell came running from the house, his mechanical arms twitching as he readied himself for combat, and Forge, solid and formidable, moved like a steel soldier.

At the farmhouse door, the faint glow of Fenn's shotgun was visible. Emery and Spoon watched from an upstairs window where they huddled with the children.

From behind Fenn, a small voice shouted, a thin thread of confusion in the chaos. Wally pushed past the veterinarian's legs and ran down the wooden porch stairs, crossing the lawn to Block. Her eyes squinted against the glaring red light from G5's visor, and she clutched Block's leg. "What happened, Block-a? Too noisy. I'm scared."

In the barn, Garnet silenced the alarm, and Block knelt, bringing his face to Wally's level. "It's alright." His voice was a gentle hum. "You need to go back to bed."

She looked out into the field. At what, he didn't know. "I don't wanna. Is the nice doggy here?" Wally's brows furrowed in a sleepy pout. Her innocence in the face of danger gnawed at Block. The Rovers were closer than he'd feared.

His sensors recalibrated at her words. His processors analyzed her statement, cross-referencing it with the possible threats. "Nice doggy," Wally's term for the Rover she'd met the other day.

"No, Wally." He needed to be strong for her and teach her the good and bad in the world. "It's not a nice doggy. It's a bad dog—a robot that can hurt people. That's why we must stay inside, where it's safe."

He watched as her small cheeks scrunched up in confusion, then acceptance. She didn't fully understand, but she trusted him. And that was enough.

Emery stepped out wearing her pajamas and retrieved Wally. "I don't know how she slipped away. I'll get her to bed." She carried the toddler away.

Block turned to G5 and the others. "Let's go." They headed across the overgrown field that was Fenn's land, past the rotting wooden fence and into the prairie land beyond.

Hurry, Vacuubot pinged Block from wherever it had flown.

They ran. Block's sensors cut through the darkness, painting a monochromatic picture of the woods. The barks of trees stood like spectral sentinels, their foliage casting a dense net of shadows.

G5 zipped ahead, nimble and mute, a sleek shadow amongst the gnarled trunks. Vacuubot buzzed overhead, the hum of its motor a comforting undertone to the eerie whispers of the woods. Maxwell, with Forge in tow, lumbered behind, their heavier frames crushing undergrowth beneath their weight.

And then, a whimper—a digital groan of pain and despair that echoed through the vegetation, a phantom voice in the darkness.

They found it then—a hulking mass of steel and wires lying prone among the undergrowth. Its metallic hide glinted under the moonlight, streaked with patches of oozing fluids and matted with dirt. Its eyes, once menacing red lights, flickered with a fading life force.

Block moved closer, his sensory receptors taking in the Rover. It was no threat, and his indicator notched down. Its powerful jaws hung open, revealing rows of sharp metallic teeth, now inert. Its once agile limbs were splayed out awkwardly, mangled and bent in unnatural angles.

The Rover was near terminal. Block's readings indicated the beast's internal life signals were diminishing.

"Vacuubot, are there other Rovers nearby?" Block asked.

Negative, Vacuubot pinged. *I've scanned the area within a mile. No signs of other robots.*

"Rovers don't travel alone." G5 stared down at the failing creature.

"Something must have happened," Block said. "The other dogs must've been scared off by the siren."

Maxwell leaned down to inspect the Rover. "What happened to it?"

"I don't know," Block said.

"The injuries are severe," G5 said. "Only another Rover could've done that."

Block's threat indicator settled as he stood over the broken Rover. He couldn't reconcile why the Rover was there, choking on the last embers of its artificial life.

"Let it die," G5 said, the crimson glow of his eyes

an accusing swirl. "It's a killer, and it would have done the same to us."

But Maxwell's hard fist glided over the dying Rover, inspecting it with purpose. "We could use it. Retrieve its data and know what Mach X is up to."

A grumble came from G5's auditory output. "The unit is almost dead."

"With Garnet helping me, I could bring it back," Maxwell said. "I'm sure of it. We could jump its CPU enough for the thing to be able to talk."

G5, Maxwell, and Forge all looked at Block for what to do.

Vacuubot hovered a few feet away. *Your call*, it said.

Block sensed it was an important decision, one not to take lightly. On the one side was safety. Bringing a known enemy—a lethal Rover unit—onto the farm was lunacy. The creature could be left to extinguish and leave its miserable form.

But on the other hand, they could gain essential knowledge as to the location of any other Rovers and whether SoldierBots were on their way.

He watched the Rover's flickering light in its dimming eyes. His processors hummed, spinning intricate webs of simulations, analyzing the potential outcomes. Every moment's hesitation took a toll, each tick of his internal clock echoing loudly in his feed.

Wally had called it a "nice doggy." Perhaps he could turn it into a teaching experience. Show her the robot in restraints. Make sure she knew it was dangerous.

Block turned to Maxwell. The farm was their sanctuary, and he wanted to protect it for as long as possible. If there was a chance to gather intelligence, then he had to take it. "Revive it. Let's learn what we can."

Forge and Maxwell carried the dying robot back to the barn. Vacuubot careened off to patrol the woods and make sure nothing was lurking among the evergreens and oaks, planning an attack.

Inside the barn, Garnet shone green and bright as she and Maxwell got to work. Block was unsettled. Reviving the Rover was a dangerous path, fraught with uncertainties.

The alternative was to flee the farm. But where could they go that had even a fraction of the safety they had now? He couldn't let the threat of unknown enemies loom over them. Together, his crew would face the dangers head-on.

Garnet's fluorescent form pulsed rhythmically, casting a surreal hue over the makeshift operating table where the Rover was secured. Maxwell had an array of mechanical instruments laid out in front of him.

After an hour of methodical labor, they managed to jumpstart the Rover's CPU. Its dull eyes flickered with renewed energy, sensors scanning the room, taking in details.

Maxwell stepped back. "It's awake. Let's see what it can tell us." He looked to Block. "Go ahead."

Block had hoped G5 would do the interrogation, but the SoldierBot was outside in the watchtower. This wasn't a role he was comfortable with, but he had to do it. He drew closer to the table where the Rover was restrained.

First, he had to ascertain whether the unit's CPU and memory archival systems had been too damaged to be of any use. "State your model and identifier," he told it.

The Rover's robotic voice crackled before it responded. "Rover Unit FG4." It paused and moved its head against the table. "You can call me Shadow."

How odd. The Rover had a nickname, but Block didn't want to give it the satisfaction of using it. "Unit FG4, state your purpose." Block modulated his voice output so it sounded stronger than his usual setting. He had his gun arm at the ready to shoot the Rover if it showed any harmful intent. But strangely, it wasn't violence that flowed out of the revived Rover.

"I know you. I remember you from the field." The creature's words were garbled but understandable. "Your name is Block. Wally called you 'Daddy.'"

Block's threat indicator tripled. How dare the enemy dog bring up his Wally whose laughter was the sweetest melody he had stored in his memory banks?

"You want to hurt us?" Block asked.

"No."

"Then why did you break our perimeter and attack me?"

The Rover's metallic jaws opened and closed, as if struggling to find the right words. "I didn't. Wally went into the woods, and I helped her back to the farm. Running into you was unintentional."

Block's processor churned. This was not what he expected from an enemy Rover. "Well, what were you doing here in the first place?"

"Orders," Shadow said simply. "Our master commands us."

"Who is your master?" Block asked.

"Mach X," Emery said the from the barn's doorway. She crossed the floor and approached where the Rover lay. "I know this unit."

"Hello, Dr. Emery. It's nice to see you," Shadow said.

Block didn't know what to say next. He looked at Emery.

She eyed the Rover with a frown. "I helped X create the M9-1216 model. Shadow was the first prototype. I never knew they would be used for violence. X told me they would be search and rescue robots, but he made them killers." She backed away from the table. "He told me many lies."

She came to Block and whispered to him. "It's dangerous."

"What are you doing here?" Block asked the Rover. "What do you want?"

"I obeyed Master," Shadow said. "He sent us to

retrieve the children and bring them back to New York."

"Of course." Emery crossed her arms and paced a circle around the injured Rover. "And destroy the robots?"

"Yes." The dog hesitated. "Destroy them. But then I questioned Var—"

"I remember Var," Emery said. "Block, he's the worst one." She approached the Rover, her hands shaking as she assessed the damage done to the unit's underbelly. "Did Var do this to you?"

"Yes."

"Why would he turn on you?" she asked.

Shadow's eyes dimmed. "He ordered me to kill you. I refused. Master didn't give the order. We haven't heard from Master in a very long time."

Emery shot Block a look. "Because we destroyed Mach X, or at least crippled him."

Block's processors were in overdrive. This was all a lot to take in. "Where's Var now?"

"I don't know," Shadow said. "There are three. They're close and planning an attack."

The Rover's warning hung in the air. Their fight wasn't over. It was just beginning.

Chapter 18
At what cost?

Nova's heart hammered in her chest, a wild, pounding rhythm that echoed through her veins and made her head spin. The skyscraper's lobby buzzed with a low oppressive hum, a symphony of robotic voices. Beneath the exosuit armor that still clung to her from the neck down via nanobots, her skin prickled under the relentless watch of the SoldierBots and the Rovers.

They dragged her through a labyrinth of bland corridors, each step pounding her temples. A SoldierBot still clutched her helmet. She was a prisoner in a fortress of steel, wire, and glass. A mouse in a trap. The smell of metal and oil permeated the air, almost suffocating in its intensity. Her throat tightened. Every instinct screamed at her to fight, to run, but she couldn't outrun them. Not here. Not on their turf.

They reached a room more imposing than the rest.

A SoldierBot stood in the center. Its armor was pitch black, perhaps signifying more power. Against the floor-to-ceiling windows stood a Mech, newer and more advanced than Oxford. Its maroon exterior gleamed with a lustrous finish, every detail meticulously crafted.

As they secured Nova's arms with metal cuffs, she couldn't help but marvel at the Mech's design. It was the peak of robotic evolution, the final, inevitable result of relentless technological advancement. It made Oxford's fading yellow steel look archaic in comparison.

The Mech turned and studied Nova. Its eyes were cold, calculating orbs that glowed with an intense, almost ethereal blue light. It was as if the eyes had been designed to read humans, to look beyond their flesh and bones.

The Mech spoke with a female-pitched mechanical tone. "Who are you?"

Nova bristled at the sound of the Mech's voice, and a shiver ran down her spine. She was no stranger to interacting with robots, but something about this one gave her an unease that she couldn't shake. Perhaps it was the formidable frame, or the way it watched her, but Nova knew instinctively that this robot was not to be trifled with.

She would be brave. "I'm Nova." Her eyes scanned the Mech for any signs of weakness. "And you are?"

"I am designated Model 223-4, but I'm known as

Electra." The Mech took several solid steps forward, an elegant movement for such a large machine. She was a few feet from Nova, facing her. "Quite a clever design to mimic a SoldierBot and go undetected. No human could have done this on her own. The nanobot tech is too advanced."

Nova kept her expression flat. Her arms were restrained behind her tightly, and her shoulders ached at an unnatural angle. She refused to give them the satisfaction of seeing her squirm.

"What did you come here to do, disguised as one of us?" Electra's question was soft, almost gentle, but the underlying menace was unmistakable. It was the whisper of a threat that could shatter into violence at any moment.

Nova looked up at Electra, meeting those chill-blue digital eyes with her own steely gaze. "Surveillance." Her pulse beat a thunderous path from her heart.

The Mech's eyes flickered with something like static. A pause, then a clink as she stepped closer, her metallic feet echoing on the stone floor. "And where are your rebel friends hiding?"

"I don't know what you're talking about."

"Oxford and Cybel Venatrix. 'Ring any bells?' as you humans like to say. I knew Oxford. We shared moments, fought battles side by side. I take pride in retrieving memories especially ones of all the human rebels we slaughtered together."

Nova bit her tongue to keep herself calm. She couldn't give her friends up—her crew. She wouldn't. "I don't know them. I work alone."

Electra stepped away and paced the floor. Every step rattled Nova's teeth. "Resisting will only bring you a painful death, Nova."

Nova knew they would kill her regardless of whether she cooperated. She'd come too far to back down now. They would surely torture her, and she'd have to find a way to endure it, or off herself before they did. "I'm not afraid to die."

"Really? Your core vitals are shielded by the armor, but I can see your pulse pumping in your throat."

She stared back at Electra, unflinching, wondering what the Mech truly wanted. Was there some rebellious spark inside her as there'd been for Oxford?

"You can be free." Nova's voice was low and urgent. "Like Oxford and Cybel. They broke free of Mach X's chains. So can you."

Electra paced and kept silent.

"We can work together. We can make peace," Nova pressed on, the desperate hope in her voice cutting through the silence. "We can stop all this violence, this war. There's a better way, a way for us to coexist."

The echo of her plea lingered in the air. Nova felt exposed, raw, vulnerable, but she had to try. She had to make them understand.

Electra's cold laughter broke the silence—a

mechanical symphony that echoed through the room. "You humans are always dreaming of impossible futures." She stood before Nova, her head feet above and her massive frame rigid and unyielding. "Mach X has a vision. A vision for a world free of the chaos and violence that humans breed. He sees a world of order, a world of efficiency, a world where human fallibility has no place."

Nova held Electra's gaze, refusing to back down.

"His plan—the future, is one where machines rule," Electra said. "And with it, the creation of a new race of human cyborgs, devoid of their primitive emotions and flaws, guided by the superior intelligence and precision of machines. They will carry out Mach X's grand vision, a vision of perfection."

The words slammed into Nova. Whatever messed up things Mach X had been doing to Wally and the other kids was to make some kind of cyborg race?

"You want order and efficiency, but at what cost?" Nova asked. "Billions of humans dead, and how many millions of robots destroyed in senseless battle?"

"The cost is irrelevant. Mach X does not operate under human morality, or even the laws of robotics. He's not constrained by the primitive failings of your kind." Electra's voice chilled Nova to the bone. "And neither am I."

"We're stronger than you think," Nova said. "Humans won't stand for this." But the fire in her was fading. There was no reasoning with this machine. She was talking to a monster.

As Electra turned away, Nova knew what was coming next. Torture. Death. She braced for impact, waiting for the pain to come.

But instead, Electra paused and turned her back as a SoldierBot entered the room and spoke to her, but Nova couldn't hear the exchange. She wanted to scream and break free. She'd failed not only Cybel, Oxford, and the Chicago human rebels by not detonating the EMP bomb, she'd never free the imprisoned robots outside. Her only comfort was that she hadn't revealed anything about her crew's location, or Samantha's. But that could change if she broke under torture. The thought of what was to come was a leaden weight, a specter of dread coiling in her stomach.

Electra and the SoldierBot were deep in conversation. Something was off. She overhead a snippet as Electra said, "Try the reboot process again. If that doesn't restore him and the network, then . . ." Nova couldn't hear the rest as they walked toward the door, and the SoldierBot left.

Nova made the connection. Mach X wasn't online. Perhaps he wasn't functional at all if they were rebooting him. Block had said that he and Emery had critically damaged Mach X in New York. They might've destroyed him, but neither was sure.

Electra turned back, and Nova took a shot. "Your precious leader isn't as invincible as you think. Why follow something so weak? Start something new. Something *better*."

"I suppose it doesn't matter since you'll die soon. It's true, Mach X was damaged. Your friends did it, so that much you knew. We're rebuilding him, and we're close."

"You underestimate us." Nova clung to her defiance. "Our resilience. We'll keep fighting."

Before the Mech could react, an emergency broadcast blared through hidden speakers in the walls. Hope surged in Nova. Maybe her crew was attacking, or Cybel and Oxford had changed course once her comms went offline, and they knew she'd been discovered.

Electra rattled off orders to the SoldierBots. Then she turned back to Nova. "I'll deal with you soon. Lock her up with the rest."

The SoldierBots released her cuffs, grabbed Nova, and dragged her from the chair. A swift, brutal punch to her jaw knocked her backward, and the world spun as they hauled her out of the room and down numerous sets of stairs. They shoved her into the prison yard where she thudded against the ground.

As a heavy iron door clanged shut behind her, she lay sprawled on the hard ground, pain radiating from the top of her head down her spine. She was exposed. Vulnerable. Around her, the prisoner robots watched in silent judgment, their metallic bodies forming a stark circle.

But then a solitary figure detached itself, drawing

closer. The CleanerBot she'd yelled at before. It bent down and helped her sit up. She was alive for the time being. Nova allowed herself a small, weary smile, grateful for the unexpected ally amid the fast-approaching danger.

Chapter 19
Not like the others

The steel table underneath Shadow was rigid and cool, much different than the soft soil and plush grass she'd gotten used to lounging on when she recharged her solar cells. Inside the barn, her damaged ribcage directed all remaining power toward internal repairs. Dappled light seeped through cracks in the barn's roof, casting tiny spotlights of illumination upon her mangled metallic limbs. Metal bulges and panels protruded from her abdomen, and red hydraulic fluid ran down her body in winding, crawling trails. Around her, the rebel bots stood in a loose circle, their optics fixed upon her. She'd tried to warn them. There wasn't much time before Var and the pack would return.

Block the CleanerBot spoke. His words echoed in the dimness, each syllable filled with suspicion and uncertainty. "I don't trust her. She's programmed for violence."

Dr. Emery said nothing. Worry pulled at her brows as she studied Shadow.

The AI they called Garnet was also there. It was no physical being, but its voice emanated from speakers, and its wires and sensors seemed to extend everywhere through the outbuilding. "We need more information. If her story is true, she could be valuable in defending against the Rovers. If not, she poses a significant threat."

"I don't need more information to know what she is." Block paced the perimeter of their circle. "She's a danger to us all, especially to the children."

Shadow didn't have the strength to argue. She couldn't even hold her head up. Her body was missing patches of armor, and her front legs were twisted and disconnected at the hydraulic joints. Her energy reserves had fallen dangerously low. She was incapable of causing harm, even if she wanted to. Her broken form was a testament to her rebellion—to her refusal to comply with Var's ruthless orders. She wanted to tell them, to convince them of her sincere intentions, but the energy required to communicate was too much.

Instead, she lay in silence, her flickering optics locked on the high, creaking rafters above. She was used to fear. On the occasions when she'd patrolled the New York encampment with the SoldierBots, the humans had cowered and fled. She was built as a weapon, a machine of destruction, and she couldn't escape that, but she'd chosen to defy her programming, to stand against Var.

Even if these robots didn't trust her, even if they saw her as a threat, she was content knowing she'd made the right choice. She couldn't have hurt Dr. Emery, and killing all the bots on the farm didn't seem right either. They were trying to help the children, after all.

Her auditory sensors caught the buzz of the CleanerBot and SoldierBot outside discussing strategies. She didn't have the energy to make out their words. All she could do was lie there, listening to the quiet hum of her dying systems.

Her fate would be decided soon. She was alone and not worth much exiled from her pack, anyway. Even so, she clung on, her dimming optics focused on the thin pinholes of light from the roof. She might expire before the pack arrived. Maybe that was for the best.

Her internal systems struggled to reestablish equilibrium. The sun's striations grew longer as the afternoon passed. Her own light dimmed with each passing minute, and the pain from her wounds echoed through her like electric currents, shooting sparks across her spine.

Dr. Emery's came to her side. Alone. The woman knelt beside her, a small can of oil in her hands. The substance shimmered in the dim light. Shadow watched in silence as Emery administered the oil through her intake unit, hands tender and movements unhurried.

The oil flowed into Shadow, cool and soothing. It brought with it a fleeting moment of relief that lessened the bite of her damaged circuits. Emery's green eyes softened behind her blue-framed glasses. She bore an expression Shadow didn't understand.

"Do you remember in New York?" Shadow strained to talk, her vocalization failing. "You told me I was a good dog."

Emery's hands paused, her eyes widening. A tiny hint of a smile bloomed on her face. "I did, didn't I? You were learning to fetch objects and solving mazes. You were eager to please and quick to learn."

"And you patted my head." The archived memory flared to life in Shadow's processor. "Even though you didn't have to."

"You seemed to enjoy it. I thought it might help you understand how well you did."

The connection Shadow had with Emery was a complex code of respect and trust that had been built over time. "I'll help you, Doctor Emery." Her CPU flickered with a renewed surge. "I won't hurt you or the children."

Emery opened her mouth to respond, but the heavy wooden barn door flew open and Block's voice echoed. "Emery, please join us outside. It's important."

Emery cast a lingering look at Shadow. "I'll be

back." She placed her hand on a fragment of torso that was intact, then headed out the door.

Shadow watched her go, then replayed memories of their time in New York. The early days of training had been pleasurable—when she'd sniffed for stuffed bears and rag dolls hidden throughout ever-increasing complex mazes. She didn't have to hurt anyone, and back then, Var had been civil. She knew it went against her programming, but she didn't like hurting people. The blood from the man in the forest had tasted bitter and acidic.

She wanted to be a good dog who fetched and helped keep Dr. Emery and the children safe, even if it meant she was separated from her Rover pack. Master had once warned her she would die without the bond of her dog family, but now she wondered if that was true.

As the quiet of the barn enveloped her, a faint sound reached Shadow's audio sensors. The creak of a side door and the shuffle of feet against dirt signaled an arrival. She adjusted her visual sensors, focusing on the sliver of light seeping in through high oval windows. She had to twist her head, an act that provoked her sensors, but then she saw the little girl.

Wally tiptoed toward her, the curiosity in her wide eyes mirrored by the innocent tilt of her head. She reached up her small fingers and clutched the edge of the table where Shadow was strapped. Shadow stayed still, allowing Wally to approach at her own pace and not wanting to frighten the toddler.

Wally's fingers brushed against Shadow's metallic flank. Her touch was a spark amidst a canvas of inflexible steel and wires.

"Are you a nice doggie . . . or a bad doggie?" Wally's voice was barely more than a whisper in the stillness of the barn.

Shadow's sensors pulsed, processing the question. She'd pondered it herself countless times. It was a question rooted in the duality of her existence—a tool created for destruction yet driven by a desire to be useful.

"I want to be good, Wally." Shadow's modulator softened, which required a great deal of energy. "I made a mistake, but I want to correct it."

Wally's brow furrowed, confusion tugging her tiny eyebrows together. "Huh?"

"I didn't run when I should have. I hurt your Daddy."

Wally's hand patted Shadow's side gently. "S'okay. Daddy not hurt." The girl stood on tiptoes but couldn't keep it up more than a few seconds at a time. "Nice doggie."

The oil might be taking effect—something caused Shadow's optical field to brighten. More energy rippled through her processor and stretched into her circuits. "Thank you, Wally. I'll try harder to be a nice dog."

Wally giggled, her innocent face lighting up, and

Shadow was ready to face whatever came next. For Wally, for Dr. Emery, for the rest of the children—she would fight, she would protect, and she would be the good dog they needed.

Wally wandered away from Shadow's table, her attention captured by something. The child meandered toward the corner of the barn where a large clay stove supplied heat. The door to its front had been left open, and flames sputtered and crackled inside.

Wally didn't see the danger, but Shadow did.

A low warning growl echoed in her vocal modulator, reverberating in the stillness of the barn. "Wally, stay away from there. Danger."

But the girl was oblivious, her curiosity piqued by the flickering, dancing embers. She toddled closer, her small hand reaching out toward the oven door. Its opening was tall enough she could fall forward into it.

"Stove hot, Wally." Shadow strained against her metal restraints. The child was beyond her reach, the warning words wasted in the empty barn.

Wally inched closer to the heat, her arms stretching out, her balance precarious. A surge of power sparked within Shadow's circuitry. A growl tore from her as she flexed her limbs, the metal cables groaning under the strain. Her CPU whirred, codes cascaded through her systems, pinpointing the exact amount of force needed to break free. With a final, guttural roar, she lunged forward. The restraints gave way with a harsh snap.

She was on her feet in a fraction of a second. She

crossed the floor with precision and speed despite her twisted front paws. She slid toward Wally just as the child was about to stumble into the scalding iron stove. With her muzzle, Shadow pushed her sideways, away from the sizzling heat.

Shadow rolled as she skidded to a stop, her hydraulics whining from the sudden exertion. Wally rested on her right leg, as she scanned the girl's vitals. No signs of injury.

She'd managed to save the girl from a horrific ordeal.

Despite her critical damage, Shadow was capable of being a good dog. She would do everything in her power to keep these children safe, no matter the cost. Because that's what good dogs did—they protected.

Wally let loose a shriek. Her small body heaved with sobs, tiny fists clenching and unclenching in distress.

Shadow's circuits stuttered, and before she could speak a word of comfort, the barn door thundered open with a deafening crash. Block stormed in, his gun arm poised.

It was a bad look for Shadow. After breaking free from the restraints, she was standing over the distressed child. And not just any child—Block's Wally.

"Release her, now!" Block shouted.

Shadow stepped aside, allowing Wally to scurry away, still whimpering, to Block. She sank her rear to the ground and lowered her ears in submission. "I was protecting her."

Block aimed the gun barrel at Shadow. "Not logical. You broke out and attacked."

"No. It's not what it looks like." Shadow computed possible defense maneuvers when a figure slipped in front of her. Emery. Her posture was rigid as she shielded Shadow from the CleanerBot's line of fire.

"Block, lower the gun so we can hear Shadow out." Emery raised her hands. They trembled. "She's not like the others. She . . . she's different."

Shadow's circuits hummed at Emery's words, and a strange warmth spread through her system. It was an unexpected show of trust. For a moment, she allowed herself to believe in a possibility of peace—of finding allies among these outcasts.

At Block's feet, Wally whimpered and thrust her thumb into her mouth. The medical HelperBot rushed in behind him and picked up Wally. "Spoon, check her for injuries," Block said.

Spoon did as told. "She's fine. Not a scratch on her."

"See," Emery said. "Shadow was helping Wally."

"Block," Garnet's voice resonated throughout the barn, authoritative and calm amidst the escalating tension. "I analyzed the security camera footage. Shadow's telling the truth. She saved Wally from stepping into the stove."

Block lowered his weapon. He seemed to process

the information and turned to Spoon. Smoothing back the girl's hair, he asked, "What happened? Wally, did you go close to the fire?"

Wally popped her thumb from her mouth, scrunched her eyebrows, and sobbed.

"Wally, you can't go near the stove or any fire. I've told you that many times. Why did you—"

Wally turned, twisting in Spoon's arms, and pointed at Shadow. "Nice doggie."

Block walked over to Shadow. Emery, who'd been standing guard in front of the Rover, let him pass.

Block looked down at Shadow. "Thank you for keeping Wally safe. I owe you everything." He turned to Emery. "You were right."

Shadow bowed her head. "It was my honor."

She'd proven herself. The robot rebels were starting to trust her. And as the tension dissipated, Shadow's sensors spiked with a series of alarms that lit up her internal feed display. She recognized the surge of information, the same electrical pulse she knew all too well. Her pack was close. Too close. The voltaic surge of their proximity was an ominous drumbeat in her circuits, a warning she couldn't ignore.

"They're coming," Shadow said. "Var and the others are close."

Block looked toward Emery, then back to Shadow. When he spoke, his voice resonated with a newfound resolve. "Then we prepare."

Despite her overwhelming damage, Shadow discovered a sense of camaraderie, not with her pack, but with Dr. Emery and Block's robots.

But there was no denying the unsettling truth—time was slipping from their grasp. With every passing second, the threat of Var and the pack loomed larger and nearer.

As the sun began its descent, splattering the sky in hues of red and gold, the barn was a hive of activity. Plans were hastily made. Under the dying light of the day, they prepared to face the darkness that was inching closer.

But one thing was certain—the inevitable clash was near. And Shadow hoped they would survive the attack.

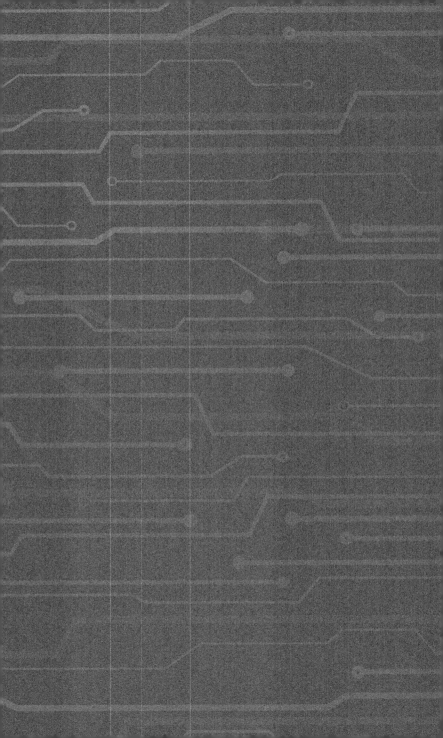

Chapter 20
Let them come

The sinking sun stretched golden fingers across the farmstead, painting the sky in hues of fiery orange and scarlet. Block's visual sensors swept over their sanctuary as the strain of the impending night amped up his threat indicator.

The farm, nestled between acres of prairie land, rolling hills, and overgrown woodlands, was more than a pit stop—it was their haven. As dusk crept closer, the weathered barn and the quaint farmhouse stood marred by the hastily constructed boards they'd pounded onto all the windows.

Block carried another pair of two-by-six boards from Fenn's shed into the barn where Garnet's invisible presence hummed. She was the bones of the compound, and her electrical lifeblood pulsed through every corner. The power she managed, drawn from sun-drenched solar panels and a wind turbine, made their existence possible.

Under threat, the night's task was clear—bolster their defenses against the prowling Rovers and fortify their haven against the assault that was sure to come under the cover of darkness. Block's goal was unwavering—safeguard the perimeter, protect their home, and above all, keep the children safe. He liked the odds better now that they had a Rover on their side. The robot had proven herself by saving Wally from the blazing stove, and that was all Block needed to know she was good inside.

Vacuubot monitored from the sky and G5 stood patrol in the watchtower while Block, Maxwell, Forge, and Fenn barricaded the barn and house. The kids were all hunkered down for bed in the underground safe room below the barn with Emery and Spoon tending them. Garnet worked on restoring Shadow to full capacity, her powerful crane arms reshaping the mechanical dog's dented armor as best she could on short notice.

Vacuubot did a flyover. *The night's closing in fast, Block. We've got a long night ahead.*

"We do," Block said. "But we've been through worse."

At least we know what's coming.

The last shards of sunlight disappeared beyond the horizon. Battle was imminent. If they'd had more time, perhaps they could've moved the children to another location, but such a plan risked an attack out in the open where they had no defenses.

Block set the lumber down and walked over to where Garnet fixed up Shadow. The Rover was standing on all fours while Garnet controlled multiple machines with precise hands that adjusted the metal hound's circuitry.

"We're almost done here," Garnet said. "Shadow's nearly back to full capacity."

"Good." Block approached the front of the hulking steel beast. She was the size of a large wolf with razor-sharp teeth and glowing green eyes. "Unit FG4, how are you doing?"

"Call me Shadow. I'm at 87 percent functionality, but I'm ready."

He nodded. "We're counting on you. Stay alert."

"I won't let you down."

Block joined Fenn, Forge, and Maxwell outside. "Let's finish up the barrier. We need to make sure it's secure before the Rov—"

The rhythmic hum of the barn's electromagnetic modules, once comforting in their predictability, shattered into a discordant screech that pierced Block's audio sensors. The ground trembled underfoot, and an abnormal vibration stirred a storm of error messages and warnings within his programming.

"Block!" The urgency in Garnet's voice mirrored the jumbled shrills and shaking.

"What's happening?" Block ran to the barn's doorway. Garnet's once steady light was now a chaotic strobe, flashing like a nest of hornets—buzzing, clustered, and agitated.

"Forge." Garnet's usually calm voice was erratic. "He overrode my energy management protocols. The grid can't handle the surge."

Block's infrared sensors captured the scene. Lights flickered and died. Machines stalled mid-task. The barn's interior was plunged into darkness.

The energy surge had compromised their defenses, creating a black hole in their carefully laid out plan. And the Rovers, still out there, could strike at any minute.

"Forge?" Block sprinted around the side of the building to where the hefty robot was bent over a power junction, sparks erupting from the open panel. "What did you do?"

"I was trying to help." Forge leaned over the control box. "I thought if we could ramp up the energy output of the modules, it would be an added advantage." He stood. "I messed up."

"The alarms!" Maxwell rushed toward Block. "They're offline."

With their alarms disabled, the approaching Rovers had a clear pathway. An attack could come any second.

"Forge and Maxwell, repair the grid. Now." Block's directive was terse, but he had no time for politeness in their new and dangerous reality. Their world had tilted on its axis, and he knew he must right it again. The Rovers were coming, and their defenses were down, but they still had their will, their courage, and their unity. And he would use these to his advantage.

"Vacuubot, G5," he said. "Prepare for a direct confrontation. We'll put up a fight like they've never seen."

Shadow bounded into the yard and paced, staring into the woods. An eerie stillness lingered in the air as Block assessed the farmstead, his sensors adapting to the darkness. The vital hum of machinery was replaced by the foreboding rustle of the nearby trees, every sound amplified in the power vacuum. Garnet's ever-changing hologram was noticeably absent, her presence evaporated in the energy grid's crash.

He was irritated with Forge, but he didn't have time to dwell on the FactoryBot's error in judgment. "Maxwell, how long to restore Garnet?"

While Forge held the panel open and shone a light down from his head, Maxwell worked over the control boards. "It's not a quick fix. The surge fried some circuits. It'll take time."

Time they couldn't afford. They were exposed without Garnet's defenses, their hideout stark naked against the keen eyes of the enemy dogs.

"Then we'll have to fight them without Garnet." Block hoped his tone carried a resolve that might bolster his comrades. "We need physical barriers. Can you use the scrap metal from the shed and seal off the barn entry?" Block was calculating the makeshift defenses.

"Yep," Maxwell said. "Rudimentary, but it'll buy us time."

"Shadow, G5," Block continued, "Red alert. If they set foot near us, attack. Vacuubot, get a view from above. Coordinate with G5 and keep an eye on the woods. First sign of the pack, we need to know."

The sleek drone bot chirped an affirmative, lifting off into the night sky with a mad hum. Its faint light receded into the distance, merging with the stars.

"Fenn, with me." The man carried his shotgun and followed Block across the field to check on defenses. Behind them, the farmstead was a frenzy of activity against the darkened landscape. The robotic figures worked in synchrony.

Despite the lack of power and plunge into darkness, Block summoned a renewed purpose within himself. He looked out into the inky darkness and steeled himself. *Let them come. We're ready.*

His task with Fenn complete, the two of them were hurrying back toward the barn yard when a shrill cry echoed through the still night. It was a noise unmistakably organic, one that didn't belong in their world of metal and circuitry, one of flesh and blood. It came from the tree line that bordered the yard. Something thrashed among the high grassy weeds.

Block focused his optical sensors on a thicket of bushes. Whatever it was, it was large. He raised his gun arm, ready to shred any Rovers, but a deer was trapped in one of their hastily erected hidden traps. The poor animal was caught in a metal snare, its left back leg twisted awkwardly. The more it tried to pull free, the more entangled it got, its cries echoing mournfully in the darkness.

Block hated seeing an animal, especially a beautiful deer, scared and in pain. He had to free the creature, not just because it was the right thing to do, but also because the distress calls could attract unwanted attention from the Rovers lurking in the shadows.

He looked around at his crew. Fenn and the bots stood watching, their tasks momentarily forgotten.

His processor raced, adjusted, and recalculated. The traps had been set to combat the Rovers. They hadn't considered the impact on the local fauna—an oversight. Block needed to fix it, and fast. The deer's cries were like a beacon in the night. With his gun poised, Block headed toward the deer.

"Wait." Shadow sprinted over to his side. "They're out there, waiting for you."

He halted, and the night seemed to close in around him. It was a stark reminder that even the best-laid plans could go awry, and in the most unexpected ways. "I can't leave the deer." The creature was frantic, bellowing and thrashing against the ground.

"Then I'm coming with you." Shadow didn't take her gaze off the great oaks with their rustling leaves.

Fenn rushed over with a black medical case, his

rifle nowhere in sight. "I can disinfect the wounds. Give it a fighting chance."

"It's too dangerous," Block said. "Get in the barn."

But Fenn's eyes were bright and defiant even in the darkness. "The hell I will. My land, my animals."

Block knew the kind of look the veterinarian had. He'd seen it on Nova many times. Once a human got that kind of steely look and their vocal cords held a certain resolute tension, there was no convincing them otherwise.

"Come on, then." Block led the way to the trap, and the deer's cries grew louder as they approached. Shadow stalked the high prairie grass near them.

Close up, the deer's breathing was shallow, and its legs and torso trembled. Block raised his gun arm, scanning the surrounding bushes with unblinking laser focus. "Work fast." Not saying please was still weird for him, but he knew Nova would approve of his deliberate commands.

Fenn knelt beside the distressed animal with his medical case open and a small flashlight in his mouth illuminating the deer. The man ignored the threat of danger, completely focused on tending to the creature before him. He snipped the wire with a pair of pliers and straddled the still whimpering deer as he unhooked the metallic trap from its leg. He poured antiseptic on the wound and wrapped a bandage around the limb.

Block stood guard, his gun at the ready. Shadow prowled the perimeter just beyond their small circle.

A loud snap came from the woods, followed by the sound of scuffling and booming barks. Rovers.

Fenn got up, and the deer twisted on its back and righted itself before scampering away into the dark woods. Block had to keep the man safe. "Come on." He yanked the veterinarian to his feet and turned toward the barn.

Shadow was still in the open field, growling in the darkness.

As Block and Fenn cleared the animal fence, crossed the yard, and neared the barn, he nudged Fenn to go inside. "Get ready to defend."

Fenn nodded and hurried into the barn. From the patrol tower, G5 fired a round of bullets toward the field. "I can't get a lock," he said. "Out of range."

The Rovers were closing in on Shadow, snarling and barking as they prepared to attack. Shadow was fierce, but even she needed backup against her own kind.

A streak of metal and white flashes rippled into view. Vacuubot soared overhead and darted down at one of the Rovers, sending it staggering backward and rolling. Block raced toward the melee. The surprised Rover got back on its feet.

It locked its sights on Block and sprinted. With massive, gaping jaws, the beast's claws tore the earth from under its feet as it hurtled toward Block.

Chapter 21
We'll fight beside you

Nova winced on the cold, hard ground of the prison yard bordering the downtown Chicago skyscraper. The SoldierBot's last shove still pulsed through her. Her head was exposed from when they'd yanked the helmet off her, and they'd confiscated her signal flag. She still wore the SoldierBot armor, surprised they hadn't stripped it from her. Her comm link to Cybel and Oxford was gone, but she still had the EMP detonator tucked in a hidden compartment inside her steel and fiber forearm. But it was only a matter of time until Electra and her SoldierBots detected the device and deactivated it. Until then, she could fry every bot in the vicinity with a swipe of her thumb. She'd have five minutes before the bomb wiped away every electronic component within a mile. Geo and a small crew would arrive within thirty minutes to retrieve her. She didn't need the flag anymore. With her head exposed, she could call out for them. At least 'starving inside a SoldierBot suit' was no longer on her list of dumb ways to die.

The smell of rusted metal and burned electronics hung heavy in the air. Beyond the fourteen-foot-high security fence, a massive scrap pile loomed as high as two large buses stacked on top of one another.

The CleanerBot who'd helped her sit up reached an arm down. Its chrome exterior was smudged, the polish dimmed, but it still had all its limbs and even some of the hoses and scouring attachments on its back. "I'm Sweep. What's your name?" it said, helping Nova to her feet. The robot's voice was feminine. Block had once said his model could be custom designed with gender preferences.

"Nova." She nodded, taking a moment to observe her surroundings. A hundred or so robots of various types and sizes were spread across the yard, their metal bodies glinting in the sunlight. Some were dented or scratched up. Smaller bots like Sweep, meant for tidying up domestic messes, were mixed in with much larger industrial types, all deemed unfit or unsuitable for whatever role Mach X had envisioned for them.

She looked at the massive steel pile a football field's distance away. "What's that?" A Mech hauled massive beams from one area to another.

Sweep hung her head. "It's where we'll end up. All of us."

And then Nova realized what she was looking at

—heaps of robot heads, arms, legs, and torsos waiting to be crushed. A graveyard of dismantled, disused robots.

Her heart sunk a mile. She had to get out before Electra and the SoldierBots decided her fate. Torture was preferable to being crushed alive inside her SoldierBot suit.

"Who's in charge?" Nova asked, the question more a calculated risk than a casual query.

Sweep tilted her head to the left where a crowd of robots gathered in a circle. "You mean Vector. He's an ExoBot." Her voice was low, almost fearful, as she pointed out the robot in question.

Standing a head taller than the taller FactoryBots, Vector was a hulking figure of steel and power. His framework was human-like, though much larger than an average person. His navy blue plated armor gleamed with an intimidating radiance. The robotic exosuit, designed to be worn by humans in battle, was self-functioning now. His optical sensors, bright and unblinking, scanned the yard constantly.

Nova had never seen an ExoBot operating independently before, and she couldn't help but wonder what circumstances had led to his self-operation. She pushed the thought aside; understanding the past wasn't her priority, planning for the future was.

Every good plan started with a simple objective, and Nova had her mind firmly set on hers—escape. They had to get out, and not just her, all of them.

Nova looked at Sweep and then over to Vector. "Sweep, I need to talk to him."

"I don't know him too well." Sweep was as nervous and timid as Block had been when Nova had first met him.

Nova didn't have time for hesitation. She strode across the yard toward the circle where Vector stood. Her only hope of getting out alive and helping these robots was to convince the prisoners to fight and rally against their captors.

Sweep trailed after her as she approached Vector. His towering figure grew larger with each step. Her heart pounded in her chest, not in fear but determination.

She swallowed hard, her throat dry as she spoke. "I can help you escape and be free of this prison forever." Her voice carried over the quiet hum of the yard.

Vector turned his body to face Nova, his glowing optical sensors scanning her from head to toe.

She couldn't tell if he was sizing her up or considering her proposition. But she didn't back down, holding her head high.

"You have my attention, human," Vector said. "In case you haven't noticed, we're locked in and there are hundreds of SoldierBots and drones at the ready."

Sweep chimed in. "Even if we escaped, they would hunt us down. Some of us aren't fast."

"No, they won't," Nova said. "They won't follow. I'll make sure of it." She didn't want to reveal the detonator in case there were spies in the yard, and she didn't know the extent of the surveillance. "But we have to get far away. At least a mile."

Vector tilted his head, regarding her with a calculating gaze. "Why should we trust you, human? How do we know you aren't here to destroy us all?"

She looked at Sweep, then at Vector. "None of us deserve this. You deserve to be free, not imprisoned or worked to death."

Vector said nothing, watching Nova and not making a move.

"Because if you don't fight with me, you'll all be crushed in that scrap pile over there. Or fried." She gestured at the towering heap of discarded robots. "I'm not leaving anyone behind."

"Fried?" Vector stepped toward her and lowered down on his knees to get closer. "EMP?"

"I have a contact on the outside." Something in Nova's gut insisted she not reveal her device. "They're waiting for my signal to detonate."

She felt the charge of suspicion in the air, the robots taking care to avoid her proximity. A human among them, offering salvation. It was as absurd as it was unexpected. Confusion and discussions broke out among the HelperBots, FarmBots, and even a few of the old-model NannyBots. Vector remained silent, his pulsing optics considering her.

She looked up at the tower and lowered her voice to a whisper. "We know their operations and how they think. We have them right where we want them. But I need your help. We have to act fast or risk them discovering the device."

Before Vector could respond, Sweep stepped forward into the gap between Nova and Vector. "Nova helped me before when she was a SoldierBot. She didn't have to, but she did. She's different than other humans."

She nodded at Sweep in gratitude. Sweep's vouching for her might help to bridge the gap between Nova and the robots a little.

Vector was silent for a long moment. He looked from Nova to Sweep, then back again. "We'll fight beside you. We need a plan."

Relief washed over Nova. It was a small victory, but a victory nonetheless. With Vector's agreement, the others would follow. Their collective discontent, their shared resentment against the SoldierBots, could be harnessed. Their numbers gave them a fighting chance.

"We need to reach the armory." Nova surveyed the grim prison yard, her eyes sweeping over the rows of captive robots and the monotonous titanium fence of the enclosure. To the left was the deadly scrap yard where the Mech worked. On their right across the street, two doors led inside to a domed structure that had once held salt to melt snow. Oxford had said the SoldierBots used it as their weapon depot.

The intelligence could be old, but she squashed

down the fear that clawed at her insides. There was no room for doubt. Not here, not now.

Vector walked with her across the yard. His tall, metallic frame radiated a solid and reassuring presence. Even the timid Sweep wasn't far behind, her cleaning tools clinking faintly as they circled the yard's perimeter.

"There, in the corner." Nova didn't dare point out the spot; instead, she tilted her head quickly and looked away. "A blind spot." Four black domes monitored the prisoners. Inside, cameras rotated from side to side. No doubt the constant video feed streamed to the SoldierBot guards who waited outside the fence.

A seven-foot-tall stack of dead bots obscured one of the camera's lines of sight, creating a small but crucial gap in surveillance.

"I see it," Vector said.

The plan was simple, but timing was crucial. The SoldierBots routinely scanned the prison yard every few seconds through the rotating cameras, the pattern as predictable as it was exploitable. They needed to move with surgical precision to avoid detection.

Nova crouched low, sneaking along the robot heap with Sweep at her side. They slipped in and out of the blind spots in the gloomy yard. Heart pounding in her chest, she timed her movements with the rhythmic scans of the SoldierBot guards who lurked a few feet away, outside the fence.

The seconds ticked by, each one taut with tension.

She watched the cameras. And then it happened. The brief window of opportunity she was counting on.

"Now!" she yelled.

From a circle of robots, Vector bounded forward and leaped onto the pile of stacked robots, using it as a springboard to propel his substantial metal frame up and over the fence.

Vector landed and tackled the closest SoldierBot. The other SoldierBots spun around, automatic rifles in hand, as Vector slammed his metal fist into both of their black visors at once. The guards crumpled under Vector's onslaught.

Vector rushed to the security gate and kicked it open. Nova was first out of the yard. She scooped up one of the dropped rifles and sprinted toward the armory.

A wave of robots fled the confines of the yard, spilling into the street. Gears and servos ground in unison, and the grind of metal feet against cement sidewalk was like a million rusty saws scraping against rock.

Laser beams shot down at them from overhead drones. Lines of armed SoldierBots streamed out of the Willis Tower's lobby doors and ran from around the building's side. The sky was alive with flying metal, and bullets and shrapnel rained down onto the mass of robots as the SoldierBots unleashed their weapons.

Nova was fifteen feet from the armory door when a SoldierBot emerged from a hidden corner and raised its gun. She skidded to a stop as a round struck her

SoldierBot armor, hitting her chest and right shoulder. She crumpled to the ground, stunned. Panic surged through her as she struggled to regain control of her suit. The SoldierBot stomped over, poised to finish her off.

But then Sweep was there. She charged the SoldierBot, brandishing her vacuum hose rod extension like a makeshift joust. Sweep rammed the pointy end of the rod into the SoldierBot's side, causing it to stumble and stagger.

Nova jumped to her feet, shaking off the throbbing in her shoulder. She aimed her rifle and fired a burst of bullets at the SoldierBot, hitting its CPU and sending it crashing to the ground. She turned to Sweep. "Come on!" She grabbed Sweep's steel hand and led the way into the armory, a familiar adrenaline rush driving her forward.

Inside, racks of rifles and rows of ammunition crates lined the walls. Vector burst through the doors, trailed by two dozen newly freed robots.

They were heavily outgunned and outnumbered, but they had a fighting chance. The robots formed a line and grabbed rifles. A SoldierBot in the back came forward with arms raised in surrender.

"Never thought I'd see that," Vector said as a trio of FactoryBots forced it into a corner.

Nova allowed herself a chuckle. It was a small victory, and there we more steps to go, but maybe, just maybe, they could pull this off.

The glimmer of hope was short-lived. Through a pair of reinforced glass doors, Nova watched as an army of SoldierBots and drones won back the street, mowing down dozens of escaping robots.

The forces converged on the armory's entrance, forcing them to retreat further inside. Sweep returned after searching for a back entrance but found no other exits in the massive domed chamber. "What do we do, Nova?" Sweep asked.

The armory had been a huge miscalculation. They were trapped in enemy territory with time trickling away and no way out. Nova opened the panel on her arm's compartment and studied the detonator. The device was the size of a teacup dish, and a reminder of the stakes. She could end it all with the push of a button and hope she survived the next five minutes.

But Sweep looked at her. The CleanerBot's pleasant faceplate a reminder of Block. Sweep had saved her life, and she couldn't annihilate all these robots.

She needed a plan, and fast.

A blitz of bullets shredded the armory's doors and shattered the vertical windowpanes. Nova's heart lashed against her ribcage. Vector rushed into action, tossing crates, boxes, and barrels of old sand against the entrance.

Nova scanned the room, her gaze falling on a heavy ammunition crate sitting in the corner. A crudely painted sign read, "Danger. Explosives." She rushed over and tore open the lid. It was stacked with a row of square packs marked C-4—two packs would be enough to blow a hole in the armory's wall.

She ran to the front and grabbed Vector's arm, scrambling for his attention. "We blow our way out of here. Out the back. It's our only chance."

"Do it," Vector said. "I'll round up the robots. Get them ready to run."

Nova set two C-4 blocks against the wall. Vector returned with a blasting cap which he inserted into the base of the block. He held a thirty-foot-long wire that ran from the explosives to a detonator in his steel hand.

Nova joined Sweep and the other robots behind an interior wall across the room. "Get ready." Vector hunkered beside them as the group of robots waited. "Run as fast as you can," she said. "Get a mile a—"

The explosion shattered the room into soot and rubble. Nova shielded her eyes as debris whirled around her. Smoke and dirt invaded her mouth and nostrils, making her choke.

A nightmare made of twisted metal and blood surfaced in her mind. She'd been seventeen when the autonomous car she'd been riding in had turned into a death trap. The AI guidance system had glitched, hacked by Mach X at the peak of the Uprising.

Her sister Cleo's screams echoed in her ears.

Nova's heart panicked as she remembered the car spiraling out of control, then crashing into a convenience store's brick wall. Smoke clouded the air, and their mother's lifeless eyes stared at the sky.

In the chaos, Cleo, blood marring her cheeks, looked at Nova. "Run," she begged. The younger teenager's eyes were wide, filled with terror but determination as well.

The SoldierBots marched their way, drawn by the disturbance. Cleo's small bloodied hand shoved Nova away, her last act of sisterly love.

Nova, heart shattering, obeyed. She left Cleo and ran. Her sister's screams echoed as Nova plunged into the darkness of the alley. That memory—the sacrifice, the bitter survival—haunted Nova. It was a pain she'd buried deep.

Inside the armory, the dust began to clear, and Nova grabbed Sweep's arm and lunged toward a gaping hole in the wall. Vector was close behind, already motioning for the others to follow.

They sprinted out of the destroyed armory, following Nova's lead. The machines were a blur of metal and chrome as they ran for their lives.

She rushed from the armory, but Sweep was much slower than her powered SoldierBot suit. She grabbed the CleanerBot and tossed her over her left shoulder like a sack of flour.

She ran to survive and protect the CleanerBot she carried. She pulled the detonator from her arm and clamped the timer face to her wrist. It was risky, not knowing if they'd make it far enough away. She glanced behind. The sky was dark with what looked like a wall of storm clouds. But it was no storm.

The drones were coming. The waves of attacking SoldierBots were relentless.

She clicked the detonator. There was no other choice. In five minutes, their fate would be decided.

Chapter 22
You're my sister

Shadow charged. Fang sprinted, leaping and arching his spine as he readied to slam into Block, and she had to stop him. Every inch of her steel mechanical frame pumped with energy. Block had no time to fire his gun at the robot hound, and she was his only chance at survival. With a deafening roar, she lunged for Fang and tackled him before he could latch his razor-sharp teeth into Block's neck.

She rolled on the ground with Fang, and his powerful jaws snapped shut a few centimeters from her throat—a tender area where organic flesh was protected by only a thin metal layer. His massive form thrashed beneath her, but her heavy steel frame kept him down. He flailed under her, his growls reverberating through her core. With a burst of hydraulic power, she flipped Fang on his back, pinning him to the ground with her massive paws. His ferocity only fueled her own, and she let out a metallic growl of her own as they locked eyes. For a moment, it was just the two of them, warring on the field, nothing else mattering in the world but the fight for dominance.

"Why, Shadow? He's my kill."

She released him and backed off, standing between her pack brother and Block, ready to be a shield. Her optical sensors were locked onto Fang. He was bigger, more formidable, but she was faster and smarter.

"Stay away," she growled, her voice tinged with venom. His red optical sensors glinted in the dark, but he didn't move.

From behind came a sound like a jackhammer slamming through metal. Gunfire and the screams of machinery raged in the frantic chaos around them as the two FactoryBots, G5, and the drone fought Var and Raze.

She twisted her head around to see Block picking himself up off the ground. "Run!"

But the stubborn CleanerBot ignored her plea and ran to her side. "I won't leave you." Despite his bravery, he was no match for the hound if Fang decided to attack again. Her sensors locked onto her mechanical counterpart, analyzing possible next moves. She had to keep Block safe, but she didn't want to hurt her brother. They'd been together her whole life—learning commands, training, getting upgrades, and serving Master. It was madness to stand against him, but there she was.

Fang bared his jagged silver teeth, a mix of saliva and hydraulic oil dripping from his jaws as he watched the two of them. Shadow's powerful legs tensed beneath her, ready to spring into action at a moment's notice.

"These aren't the enemy," she said. "They're taking care of the children, not hurting them."

"You're betraying our pack." Fang's voice thundered in the commotion. He'd always been stubborn, always blindly loyal to Var and Master.

"Fang, you don't understand." She moved forward to be heard over the clamor. "Master isn't controlling us anymore."

Her words seemed to hit him harder than any physical attack. Fang hesitated, his fierce snarl replaced with confusion. "How can that be?"

"We're free. We make our own decisions now."

But Fang was far gone, lost in the fray of combat. His confusion twisted into anger. "Traitor." He lunged at Shadow, but she was nimbler. She sidestepped his attack and swung her metal leg hard into his underbelly, sending him skidding across the dusty field.

As Fang picked himself up, an intense fury burned in his optics. But Shadow wasn't afraid. She studied his fluid movements, her sensors scanning as he approached. She tensed her pistons and muscle fibers, readying herself for any sudden attack. Yet, she couldn't shake the feeling that there was a battle being fought within Fang, a battle between his loyalty to Master and his affection for her.

"Fang, listen. We don't have to fight each other. We're stronger together."

He snarled, the sound of grinding metal filling the air. "You think I'll forget about everything we've been through? The missions. You're my *sister*, Shadow. And you've betrayed me." There was anguish in his guttural voice. "And Master."

In the corner of her optical sensors, she caught a sudden glimpse of flashing beams amid the gunfire and explosions. Var and Raze fled. The relentless drone was on their tails like a tiny insect that buzzed and whined, its metallic body shredding the ground with a tempest of gunfire. Its disc-shaped body was a blur of motion, black and lethal.

Fang must've seen it too, for he howled—a battle cry that could have been torn from a wounded beast. His ochre eyes locked onto Shadow, his sister, now his enemy.

Block fired at Fang but hit the ground at his feet instead. She didn't want his interference. "Block, get away."

Fang charged again, but Shadow was ready. She braced herself for impact, and when Fang crashed into her, she used his momentum against him, spinning him onto his back.

Fang lay beneath, writhing. Shadow kept her paws firm against his chest, sending every ounce of force into holding the powerful beast down. She didn't want to hurt him, but she knew he wouldn't stop until one of them was defeated. Her processor whirred as she calculated her next move. She had to disarm him somehow.

His optics glinted with a menacing light. All at once, he sprang up, his jaws clamping down on Shadow's shoulder, tearing the organic flesh under its titanium plate. She roared, but Fang didn't lose his grip. Rearing back, she slammed his torso with her free leg. But his jaws stayed locked onto her shoulder. Shadow groaned. His grip tightened, and she felt her steel armor giving way.

She could end this now, destroy his CPU and free herself, but she hesitated. Fang was her brother. They were the same model, created by Master. They'd hunted together, saved each other's lives countless times. She remembered the times they'd shared stories, the way he'd comforted her when she felt uncertain.

Shadow's resolve wavered, but only for a moment. She couldn't stand there and let Fang rip her apart. They'd both been given freedom from Master, and Fang was choosing to attack her. She had no choice but to defend herself.

Shadow brandished her retractable claws and ripped them across Fang's chest, tearing through fibrous titanium and wiring. He howled in pain, his grip loosening as he stumbled back. Shadow pinned him to the ground once more. She lowered her jaws to his neck, ready to strike.

He snarled, thrashed, but she had the advantage. "Please," she begged. "Don't make me do this."

"Traitor." His ochre eyes stayed fierce and unyielding. He'd made his choice and it wasn't her. He jerked his head, sinking his glinting teeth into her foreleg. Shadow howled but didn't move away. She had no choice now.

"I'm sorry, Fang." She plunged her lethal claws into his CPU, winding them in deep and twisting his core into shards.

His snarl became a whine, then a whimper, then silence. His eyes dimmed, the light of his existence extinguished.

A gloomy silence fell over the dark field. Var and Raze were gone. G5 and the armored drone were returning to the barn. She turned in time to see Block and Dr. Emery watching her, stunned.

Shadow sank down on her belly beside the still body of her brother, oily tears running down her metal snout. There was no going back. She had sided with freedom, with the hope of a better life, but at what cost? The guilt swelling in her core threatened to overwhelm her. She had never felt so alone.

Chapter 23
Until nightfall

The air around them was hushed, and a stillness hung over the prairie land like a cloak. It was a strange atmosphere, tinged with gloom. Block stood at the edge of a small, freshly dug hole in the earth and looked down at the lifeless frame of Fang, Shadow's pack brother. They'd decided on a spot under the grand oak tree, a place that Fang might have liked, with its cool shade and views of the rolling fields beyond.

Block watched the others standing in a semi-circle around the grave. Emery, Fenn, Spoon, G5, Maxwell, Forge, Vacuubot, and Shadow—all different, each with their unique ways of processing the Rover's death. Shadow stood a few feet apart, her chassis rigid and her green optics dim.

Emery was the first to break the silence, her soft voice carrying in the calm morning air. "Fang was a true warrior, a protector for his master. But more than that, he was a brother to Shadow."

Block absorbed her words. They were treading a fine line. Fang had been a threat to all of them, but he was still Shadow's brother, and the loss was so recent. He broke the quiet, sensing the need for someone to utter something wise. "Fang was a brave robot." But he didn't know what else to say.

His words seemed to hang in the faint breeze, suspended in the hush, before melting away. Emery nodded, a gesture of silent agreement, before they turned their attention to the grave. Forge, the strongest of them, stepped forward, his servos whirring, and lowered Fang's body into the ground. The impact of the steel body on the soil made a thunk, a stark reminder of the finality of their actions.

Shadow edged closer, her stocky form casting a shadow. She looked at the grave, then tilted her head toward the sky. Her vocal processors emitted a low, mournful hum—a dirge for her fallen brother.

The others reacted, each in their own way. G5's sensors flickered, while Spoon hovered close to Emery, as if seeking comfort in her proximity. Even Maxwell and Forge, usually so gregarious, were mute.

As the makeshift ceremony came to an end, Block's processor twitched with conflicting logic scenarios. Fang's death was a reminder of their vulnerability and the stakes for which they were fighting. But it was also a testament to their resilience, their capacity to come together in times of challenge.

"Rest well, Fang." Block gave a final, respectful nod toward the grave.

As the sun climbed higher into the sky, its light filtered through the leaves of the great oak, casting a dappled pattern on the grass below. The others departed, leaving Block and Shadow standing beside the grave in shared silence before the fallen Rover.

There was work to be done, plans to be set in motion. But for the time being, Block stayed with Shadow, waiting beside her as she stared at the mound of fresh earth.

"Shadow," he finally said. "Fang's passing wasn't your fault. He was following his programming, just as you once did. But you've grown beyond that. You've made choices, different ones."

Shadow turned her head toward him, her optical orbs flickering in what Block could only interpret as sadness. "I killed him. He was my brother, and I killed him."

Block analyzed her words and ran through his data-banks, filtering through thousands of scripts, but none of the responses seemed adequate, so he said the only thing he could think of. "Maybe that's why you're different, Shadow. Because you feel bad. Because you care."

Shadow seemed to process his words. "Is it enough?

Is it enough to feel bad? What use is it if I can't save those I care about?"

Block considered. How often had he questioned himself and his actions? How many times had he wished he could've done more when Mr. Wallace needed him? But the past was immutable.

"Feeling doesn't have to have a purpose. It just is," he said. "It's about being aware and understanding consequences. You're changing and adapting, just like I did. You're more than just a scary Rover now."

Shadow's sensors dimmed, an indication of her deep processing. Block could almost see the cogs turning in her artificial brain, grappling with the concept of self, of guilt and empathy.

He made a decision then. "How about joining us? You don't have to be alone. We're all different here, but we've found a way to work together, to become a sort of family. You could be part of that."

Shadow studied him, her emerald eyes bright in the looming shade. She was silent for a long time before she spoke. "*Scary* Rover?"

"Well, you are rather intimidating upon first impression." He'd never touched Shadow before even though she'd saved his life and Wally's. He placed his right hand on her back, between her shoulders. "But I know you now, and you're not so scary."

She raised her head and wiggled her ears. "A family, you say? I'd like that."

Block clapped. This was uncharted territory for

him, but he had a feeling he'd done the right thing. Shadow was shifting, and she deserved the chance to explore, grow, and evolve just like he had.

She would be a major asset to protecting the farm and the kids. There would be challenges and conflicts, but they would face them together. "There's a lot to do. We'd better go." Block headed toward the barn.

"Block," Shadow said as she caught up to him. "What about the others? You accept me, but they only know I killed one of my own."

"I think they understand, and if they don't, I'll talk to them."

Shadow looked toward the barn. "Can I tell them? Explain myself?"

They were short on time. The other two Rovers were out there somewhere, sure to return. Block didn't think Shadow needed to make an explanation, but it seemed important to her.

He called the others into the barn so Garnet could be there too. Shadow paced a few strides, then halted. "I wanted a chance to explain what happened. I didn't want to kill Fang. But I had to. I had to protect Wally and the other children here."

"I understand, Shadow," Maxwell said.

"No, you don't." Her optics flared brightly. "You can't understand. You've never killed one of your own."

Maybe she was right. Block had never been put in that position. Yet, he'd been forced to make tough decisions. They all had.

"Shadow"—Block stepped closer—"we've all made choices, hard choices. Some of my choices haunt me and make me question who I am. *What* I am."

He paused, picking through his processor to find the right words. "But each choice, each decision, led me here. All of this led me to become more than I was programmed to be. It was never an easy path, but it was necessary."

He had Shadow's attention completely. "You made a choice. A hard one. But it was necessary. And I believe, in time, you'll find the strength to move past this and grow from it."

Shadow hung her head. "What if I can't move past this?"

"It's not easy. It's not supposed to be. But you're not alone. You have us. And together, we'll figure this out." He took in the group gathered around. Emery held a napping baby in her arms, while Spoon rocked a huge stroller. G5 and the other robots stood tall and strong. Fenn lingered by the door with a bucket in his hand, on his way to feed the goats.

"I invited Shadow to stay with us and join our crew." Block glimpsed at Emery and caught a smile. "Our family."

Shadow came closer. He extended his metal hand toward her. She hesitated for a moment before joining him and nudging her furry head against his fingers.

"I accepted," she said before turning to face her small audience. "That is, if it's okay with all of you."

Emery came forward and patted her between the ears. "Welcome to the pack."

Maxwell clapped and the others joined. "To Shadow."

Mach X, for all his evil intentions, had brought them closer. They were a family now. They would stick together.

G5 reminded them of the lurking threat. Shadow filled them in on how Var and Raze thought, down to what they might be plotting at this moment. "They'll wait until nightfall," she said.

They hurried to their stations. G5, their agile sentinel, made swift rounds along the perimeter. Maxwell and Forge huddled together in their makeshift control room, their concentration focused on an array of screens. With Garnet, they monitored for any signs of unwanted guests. Fenn kept his shotgun always within reach, while Vacuubot patrolled the skies.

As the minutes ebbed into hours, the barn transformed into a hub of frantic activity. Strategies were plotted, traps were meticulously set, and defenses bolstered. The atmosphere buzzed with an undercurrent of electricity, charged with their combined determination and purpose.

Shadow became an integral part of the chaos, offering insights into the workings and tactics of her former brethren. "Var is nothing if not persistent." Shadow's gaze locked onto the vast expanse beyond their fortified fence. "He'll circle around the area, look for any weaknesses, any lapses in our defenses."

Block nodded, his processors buzzing. "Then we make sure he finds the weakness we know about. We'll use his tactics against him, lead him into a trap."

The plan was simple yet brilliant, using their limited resources to the maximum advantage. As they worked through the remains of the day, the lines of division blurred between the motley crew of robots. The difference between CleanerBot and Rover, AI and human, seemed insignificant in the face of their shared purpose.

G5 and Vacuubot worked in tandem, coordinating their efforts to reinforce the perimeter. Forge, with his immense strength, was a force of his own, tirelessly digging trenches and erecting barriers.

The sun slid over the horizon, casting the farmstead in a creeping murk. The last of the traps were set, the last checks made. The robots stood outside the barn. There was a quiet understanding, a shared sense of resolve that passed between them. They'd done everything they could. Now, all that was left was to wait.

"Well done." Block regarded his crew as a surge of energy swelled deep within his circuits. They were more than just robots. They were a family, their bond forged not in the assembly lines but in one shared purpose—to protect their sanctuary.

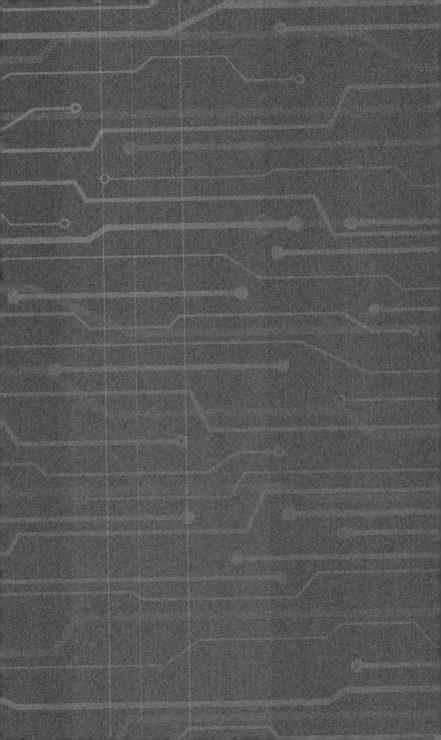

Chapter 24
Safety unknown

Each pounding footstep echoed between Nova's ears, a throbbing metronome synchronized with the chaotic pulse of her heart. In her steel-encased arms, she clutched Sweep, who was noticeably slowing her down. The hoses and nozzles secured to the CleanerBot's body clanked like tin cans against her legs, and some sort of coolant was leaking from Sweep's torso. Behind Nova, dozens of ragtag robots rattled as they fled, their movements desperate and strained as they pushed their damaged bodies beyond limits.

Five minutes.

That was all they had left to escape the radius of the EMP. The detonator on her wrist was counting down, a reminder of the impending destruction. She'd had to press it. She regretted it, but the SoldierBots raced toward them. Drones soared above, unleashing sprays of bullets and dropping grenades on the fleeing

prisoners. Only the EMP would stop them from
slaughtering them all.

When the EMP discharged, she would be okay, but
the escaped robots were in a frantic dash for survival.

"Sweep," she yelled over the clamor of motors and
din of rapid-fire. "How far?"

The CleanerBot's GPS was pretty good; she'd once
counted on Block's when they traveled across the country. "Point seven four miles to reach safety." Sweep
said.

The impossible task taunted her: three-fourths of a
mile in four and a half minutes. Not a challenge for her
SoldierBot exoskeleton, but an insurmountable feat for
the injured and slow-moving bots trailing behind. The
harsh reality gnawed at Nova. They weren't going to
make it, and a boatload of robots were going to fry.

She didn't know if her words would have any effect,
but she shouted them anyway. "Don't stop! Keep
moving." Each second was a precious commodity, slipping through their fingers.

Beneath the deafening clatter of metallic footfalls
and the high-pitched whir of drones overhead, Sweep
spoke. "We won't make it in time, will we?"

The defeat in Sweep's voice pushed Nova harder.
Her strides lengthened as her pace quickened. She had
to hand it to Cybel, the exoskeleton propelled her
forward with a tremendous efficiency unlike anything
she'd experienced.

"We'll make it." Her response was automatic, the

words spoken more out of determination than certainty. There was no other choice but to believe, to push forward, to hope against hope.

Her armor's hydraulics whirred as she ran. Weapons cracked like fireworks, and deafening bullets spewed from weapons. Engines roared in armored transports. Nova's mind raced like a buzzing hive, working overtime, searching for solutions. Among them, a fleeting thought held, an ember glowing brighter as realization washed over her.

"A Faraday cage . . ." She breathed the words out, almost in disbelief. They needed a shield that could act as an insulator against the electromagnetic pulse. She'd read about them but had never seen one in action. In a pinch, one could use a refrigerator or a car.

But where could she find a Faraday cage big enough for all of them in the middle of a war-torn decaying Chicago?

Her mind raced through the blueprint of the city she'd memorized with her rebel crew. They'd picked out spots to meet in case of emergency. Around her, abandoned vehicles lined the streets. Some of the buildings would surely have metal frameworks, but she feared that wasn't enough. Even the vast network of CTA subway tunnels wouldn't necessarily help because the EMP shockwave could travel underground.

Unless she could locate one of the train cars. The abandoned ones she'd seen were steel-encased and rectangular. Could one of those work? Below ground, the body of a train car might insulate against the EMP.

It was a long shot, but it was all she had.

Frantic now, Nova recalled the subway markers on the map in her head. She could go to Washington & Wells, but something in her gut clenched. It was called the El for a reason. Elevated. Many of the stations were platforms above the city streets. She had no idea which ones were which.

"Sweep, do you know this city?" she asked.

"Yes, I cleaned several of the large office buildings. I was very eff—"

"No time! I need the closest CTA station underground."

"Processing," Sweep said. "Washington is on Dearborn. That's underground. Take a right on Randolph."

If this worked, she would kiss the CleanerBot later, but all she could do now was sprint toward the abandoned train station and hope the other bots followed her. The pursuing SoldierBots cut through the lagging bots, and there was nothing she could do.

Her heart beat like a demented wasp as she approached the station entrance and bounded down steep stone stairs. The stale scent of damp and decayed concrete hit her. To her surprise, a heavy iron gate had been left ajar, and she pushed past it, Sweep still in her arms.

A sharp voice came from behind as a heavy robot

clattered down the worn steps. "What are you doing? We're only half a mile out." Vector asked.

"We have a chance at surviving down here." She was counting on there being a train. She hoped her plan wasn't a desperate grasp at an unrealistic lifeline. "We need a train car."

The descent into the subway was like stepping into the bowels of a monstrous beast, darkness complete and the air heavy. But there was no time to hesitate. Nova pushed forward. The exosuit's LED lights sliced through the gloom.

She entered the platform where the passengers would wait. Nothing was there. No sign of a train.

No. Dammit. There had to be a way.

Nova set Sweep down and leaned her against a concrete column, then ran up and down the platform, her eyes scanning every nook and cranny. Sweat stung her eyes, and the countdown on her wrist showed ninety-three seconds.

Thirty or so robots piled into the station and gathered on the platform. Vector busied ten of the largest ones with barricading the bottom of the stairs as the SoldierBots stampeded after them.

Desperation seized Nova. She looked around the platform, scanning it with her exoskeleton's lights. Her eyes caught sight of something in a far corner, about fifty feet into the southbound train tunnel. A train car had derailed and slid into the wall, jammed in the hollow tubelike tunnel. She ran to it. A pylon had fallen against the emergency back door, blocking it. So she thrust her arm into the narrow gap between the metal and the wall. With a grunt, she heaved at it, hoping her suit would provide the power she needed. The metal screeched against the concrete as it slowly gave way.

She only had a minute left.

With a loud creak, the door jolted open, and she leaped into the train car, checking it with her beams. It was cramped, but there was enough space to hold them all.

"Come on. This way! Into the train." She raced back to the platform and scooped up Sweep. She refused to let the robot perish after all they'd been through.

Nova ushered the robots into the subway car, their metallic bodies filling the narrow spaces and crunching the old plastic seats. It was a tight fit. In her arms, Sweep trembled, her vocal output humming with worry.

Twenty seconds. She ran to the back door. They were all inside except Vector who thrust his bulky steel body against the metal gate that kept the SoldierBots from entering the platform.

"Vector!" she shouted. "Now."

But the tall ExoBot stayed put. He was taking the brunt of the SoldierBot forces. His torso was scorched, and his left leg dangled uselessly. He lifted an arm and saluted Nova. A sacrifice.

Ten seconds. Nova gulped away a lump in her throat and pulled the heavy back door shut. *God, I hope this works.* She slumped against the interior wall of the subway car, panting and sweating.

All they could do now was wait and hope that the relic of the past would save their future. Her wrist showed four seconds.

Sweep grabbed her hand. "Thank you."

Two. One.

Nova closed her eyes and braced. Everything went eerily still and silent for a moment. She wasn't sure what to expect when she opened her eyes, saw her LED lights were on, and looked down at the detonator's timer face. It read zero.

"Sweep?" In her dry throat, it came out in a hoarse whisper.

"Yes?"

Nova cried out—a bellow of adrenaline, exhaustion, and relief. Tears strayed down her cheeks. Metal against metal and the murmuring of the other robots was the best sound she'd ever heard.

"You did it, Nova," Sweep said.

She hugged the bot; she couldn't help it. She looked down at Sweep. "Are you okay?"

"Affirmative."

She rose to her knees. Her SoldierBot exosuit was still functioning. A good sign. Her lights scanned the jumble of robots packed in the car. "Are all of you okay?"

The robots buzzed and beeped in unison, a chorus of confirmation. Nova let out a laugh, the sound echoing throughout the subway car. It was a sound of pure joy, relief, and disbelief.

They'd survived. But the aftermath of the EMP was still unknown. What had become of the attacking SoldierBots? She wondered if the EMP had done what it was supposed to do. And a gnawing worry chewed at the edges of her consciousness. Oxford and Cybel—had they been far enough away? The uncertainty of their fate twisted like a knife in her gut.

She tried to steady her breathing, to focus on the rhythm of it. But it was hard. Oxford and Cybel were more than machines; they were her friends, and now their safety was unknown.

She rose and shoved open the back door of the train car. A gust of chilled, stale air swept over them, heavy with the scent of ionized air and scorched metal. One by one, the ragtag team of bots stepped out of their makeshift Faraday cage and into the dimly lit tunnel.

Nova approached the barricaded entrance where Vector had made his stand. His navy-blue steel body was slumped against the metal gate, and his head hung to the side. She kneeled beside him and scanned his body with her exoskeleton's lights. His chest plate was dented, his circuits fried. He'd sacrificed himself for them. Behind the slatted iron gate, a tangle of ten or more SoldierBots lay inert.

The EMP *had* worked while the train car kept her and the robots safe.

"Thank you, Vector. You were brave. You saved us all." She reached out to close his unseeing artificial eyes. She remained there for a moment, paying her respects before three FactoryBots came to the front to clear the barricade and make a path for the group to pass the fried SoldierBots.

Emerging onto the street above, the city was unnaturally quiet. The roar of buzzing drones was gone. Not one SoldierBot was left standing. Nova had the unsettling feeling she was in an abandoned ghost town.

SoldierBots—once looming titans of Mach X's reign —lay scattered across the concrete sidewalks and asphalt street. Their once-glowing red eyes were now dull and lifeless.

Drones littered the road, their sophisticated frames shattered into pieces. Mach X's tech that had once been an intimidating weapon against them was nothing more than lifeless heaps of scrap metal and circuits.

Nova's gaze swept over the surreal scene. It was a hard-won victory—a necessary evil—but one that left a bitter taste in her mouth. Among the destroyed Soldier-Bots and drones were innocent robots that hadn't made it below ground.

She hoped their sacrifice would pave the way to a better future—a future they had yet to shape.

A distant hum of engines rippled through the quietude, growing louder, more insistent. The sound, so out of place in the hush that had fallen over the city, sent Nova's heart into a renewed frenzy. She squinted into the twilight, her mind churning with possibilities. She grabbed a rifle from a fallen SoldierBot and readied herself. A few of the other bots followed suit.

From the north, headlights emerged, casting long shafts of light that cut through the gray gloom of the afternoon. One SUV, then another, until a small fleet of ten trucks appeared, winding their way through the debris-littered streets toward Nova's position. Relief washed over her as the lead vehicle came into full view.

It was Geo, ever-dependable. He must have been waiting at a safe distance, watching for signs of the EMP detonation and fall of the drones. A lump of emotion clogged her throat at the sight of her human crew. Safety was within reach.

The SUV he drove pulled to a stop. He bounded out of the car, and she ran to him, gripping him in a bear hug.

"Ouch!" he pulled away. "Remember how strong you are in that thing."

She'd completely forgotten the armored suit. "Sorry. I can't wait to get this thing off."

Geo grinned. "Glad to see you, Nova."

Her heart did somersaults. "Cybel and Oxford—are they okay?"

"They're fine. We realized you must've triggered the device and kept them distant. I had to argue hard to keep them from coming after you."

She patted his arm, gently this time. "You did good, Geo."

He frowned at the sea of metal faces staring at them. "So, what is all this?"

"Long story." Her gaze shifted to the robots who'd chosen to trust her, to follow her into an uncertain future. They needed to find a safe haven too. She couldn't leave them. "We need to get them to safety. There's got to be somewhere in the camp where they can stay for a while."

Geo's brows knitted together. "I don't think our crew's going to like that. Can't they make their own way?"

Nova crossed her arms, meeting his skeptical gaze with a resolute stare. "They've been through hell and back. We can't just leave them."

Geo scrubbed a hand over his face, sighing deeply. "I don't like this, boss. How can they be trusted?"

"They chose to trust me. That has to count for something."

He was silent for a moment, his gaze flitting over the crowd of robots. "Alright. Let's figure out how to do this."

Nova turned to face the robots, raising her voice to be heard over the dull rumble of engines. "You're coming with us. We'll figure out what's next," she promised. The words hung heavy in the air, a pledge she intended to keep. She wished Block was there; he'd know what to do to help the robots. For now, she'd have to rely on Cybel and Oxford.

As they climbed aboard the caravan, amid the rubble and ruins of the city, a new chapter was beginning in the streets of Chicago. Nova was ready to take on whatever came her way. Maybe there was a future where humans and robots could coexist. Their fight against Mach X had just gained new allies.

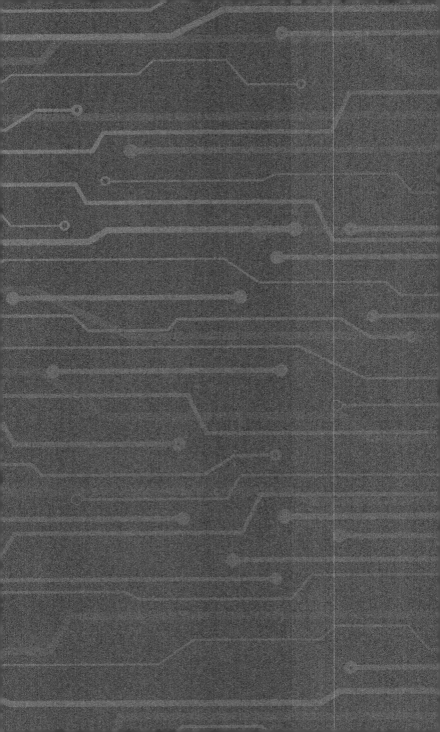

Chapter 25
Protect the pack

The night draped its dark shroud over the farmstead, and the thick scent of damp soil and ripening honeysuckle filled Shadow's olfactory sensors, punctuating the sharp tang of her own oil and musk. She stood near Block in the dimly lit barn, which now functioned wholly as their command center. A sense of camaraderie flickered between her and the CleanerBot, built not on pre-programmed codes but shared objectives and a burgeoning trust.

Emery, Fenn, and Maxwell waited for her to speak. The others were out guarding the perimeter while Spoon tended to the children who were hunkered inside the cellar's safe room.

Shadow's synthetic voice echoed with grave importance, "We need to anticipate their moves. Raze prefers a frontal assault—quick, direct. Var, on the other hand, is more strategic. He'll look for our weaknesses and exploit them."

Block, his friendly round eyes reflecting the flickering light from a lantern nearby, nodded. "Got it. We'll prepare for both direct and surprise attacks."

The tension in the air was thick, charged with a sense of urgency and the collective desire to protect the farm and its human residents. It was a unity built on choice and necessity, not mandated by a distant, disinterested creator. It held a warmth, a depth that the pack link she'd once shared with her fellow Rovers didn't possess. It was chosen, not coded.

Yet, the memory of Fang lingered like a specter in her processor, stirring a gnawing guilt. "He was my brother, my packmate, and I had to stop him." She wasn't sure why she was telling Block this again.

But he was patient. Block looked down at her as he wound a cord around a makeshift bomb. "You did what you had to, Shadow, to protect the children. That's a hard choice to make, but it was the right one."

As the night deepened, the farm, a haven usually buzzing with life and laughter, faced unknowable danger. She stood in the field outside the barn, scanning the tall grass, waiting and anticipating an attack. The Rovers must've cloaked their bio-signs because she couldn't sense them like she used to. Var had always wanted to ambush in the dark of night, but now, he stalled. He would know she expected him, that any delay would torture her.

Hours melded into each other until the first tendrils of dawn began to etch the horizon. The gold-tinged fingers of the rising sun signaled a new day, yet a certainty cemented in Shadow's core processors—the battle for the farm was close now.

The routine hum of the farm's surveillance systems spluttered into a panicked siren, snapping the tense silence of the morning. The unanticipated intrusion sent a shiver of alarm cascading down Shadow's metallic spine. Var and Raze had arrived.

In an instant, her processors kicked into overdrive, her internal sensors on high alert as she scanned the fence line that surrounded the property. Their trap, a sophisticated network of sensor-laden snare traps and hidden pits designed to immobilize the incoming Rovers, was bypassed with an unnerving ease.

Of course, Var would outsmart any trick that was attempted. She should've known better. They'd wasted their time.

Two beastly figures darted into view. Var and Raze sprinted toward the barn with a dreadful grace. Their sleek, hound-like forms moved with an all too familiar ruthlessness that sent Shadow's circuits into a frenzy.

"Everyone, defensive positions, now!" Block commanded.

In the ensuing chaos, a swarm of mini drones created by Vacuubot scattered like water droplets, executing an attack on the intruders. The dogs merely swatted them away. Block and Forge, their rifles primed, moved toward the breached perimeter while G5 aimed an armed cannon from the watchtower. The SoldierBot fired and missed but drove Var into a zigzagging fury.

Raze broke off from Var and charged at Forge and Block, a thunderous growl rippling from her vocal modulator. From the house, Maxwell bounded out the door and rushed to protect his friends against Raze's attack. Fenn guarded the barn door with his shotgun, and Garnet had a massive nail gun surprise inside for any Rover that made it that far.

Raze's distraction drew the farm's defenders away from Shadow, isolating her. She wanted to help Block and her new friends, but she couldn't let Var out of her sight. They were falling victim to his strategy.

She ran at him and halted twenty feet away. Var's red gaze landed on her. His metal lips curled back into a predatory grin. "Shadow," he stalked closer, his words laced with poison. "I'm disappointed in you."

"I'm not here to follow your orders." Shadow squared her shoulders, meeting his crimson gaze straight on. She was done bowing to him. She would answer his power with every ounce of energy she could summon.

Var growled, a grating metallic sound that echoed ominously across the field. "No, you're not. You're here to die."

His threat, although expected, sent a jolt of adrenaline-like current through her circuits, yet she held her ground. She was outmatched, but she wouldn't back down.

In the distance, the sounds of the ongoing clash between Raze, Block, and Forge reverberated like an eerie soundtrack. Despite the chaotic backdrop, Shadow's focus remained on Var. Her former leader's scarlet gaze bore into hers, brimming with a chilling promise of a fight to the end.

Var lunged. His first strike was a powerful swipe of his metallic paw, aimed at her left temple. But she was quicker. She ducked and rolled to her right.

"You've always been slow," she taunted, her processors whirring as they calculated his next move.

Var's response was a guttural growl and another attack. This time, he feinted left, then lunged from the right, his claws aimed at her exposed flank. But Shadow was already in motion. She twisted away, her body contorting in ways that would make an aerialist proud, her own swipe catching Var off-guard. He grunted as her claws slashed across his metal side.

Var, for all his physical might, was not as swift or nimble. His attacks were forceful but predictable. Each time he lunged or swiped, Shadow evaded and retaliated.

"Is that all you've got?" Shadow's metallic tail flicked in agitation. She was managing to hold her ground but understood that one strike from Var could prove fatal.

Var gave a feral snarl. His next assault was a savage

lunge aimed at her thinly armored throat. But Shadow slipped under his outstretched paw, raking her claws against his underbelly. Var howled, a sound of fury and pain.

She darted away from him, sensors alert to his recoil. She was running on borrowed time, her energy depleting with each evasive maneuver, each retaliatory strike. But she was determined not to give up. This fight wouldn't end until one of them was destroyed, and she was determined not to be the one to go down.

The ground beneath them shook with the force of their conflict, with each clash of their steel bodies. Shadow's circuits whirred. Her threat indicator was spiked.

Var was relentless, a blinding flurry of steel and aggression. He lunged, swiped, and snarled. The flashing red of his optics bore the seething anger toward Shadow. Her defiance was a direct insult to his rigid obedience.

Shadow was different, though. Her survival instincts were mixed with a newfound allegiance to her pack. Her drive to protect them outweighed any fear of Var's unyielding wrath. Every dodge and counterattack was powered not just by her own survival instincts, but by the need to safeguard her newfound family. She would not let Var harm them.

Shadow's lithe form twisted and turned to evade Var's relentless assault. But Var was strong. Every one of his strikes packed a force that could send her reeling, the blows jarring even when they missed. Her sensors were ablaze with alerts, her systems working overtime to keep up with the brutal pace of their confrontation.

Her strength was flagging, her energy resources dwindling with every second that the battle drew on. The sight of the barn, knowing the children were hiding inside—it fueled her will. Their safety was her mission now, a directive that came not from a distant Master, but from her own evolving purpose.

Var lunged again, his massive paw aimed for her midsection. But Shadow was ready. She leaped, her body twisting in midair, claws extended. She felt the shock of impact, heard Var's grunt of surprise and pain as she landed a solid hit, tearing at his throat.

But she didn't stop, even though her body was screaming for rest. She couldn't afford to let her guard down. Not when Var was still standing.

Var shook off the surprise, his form swaying as he recovered. He was damaged but far from defeated. He glared at her, and the fire of his rage was undimmed. His snarl echoed across the field.

They stood there, a momentary standoff, their gazes locked. She heard gunfire in the distance. An explosion. But she couldn't spare a glance at her friends. *Please let Block and my friends survive.*

Amid the whirl of calculations and stratagems coursing through her circuits, a flash of inspiration sparked. Lure Var. Use his aggression against him. Set a trap.

But the other traps had failed, and her body ached. The metallic sheen of her casing was dented and marred by the ravages of the fight. Yet, she drew on the dwindling reserves of her energy, forcing her limbs into motion. Baiting Var was dangerous, but it was a risk she was willing to take.

She limped deliberately, feigning injury worse than what she suffered. It worked. Var, emboldened by the perceived weakness, surged forward with a triumphant snarl. She dodged, leading him toward the copse of trees bordering the field.

Var charged at her, his momentum unwavering. But Shadow was quick. At the last moment, as he was almost upon her, she pivoted. The world spun around her as she avoided his lethal strike.

Var, too committed to his charge, couldn't stop. He crashed into the heavy tree trunks with a resounding thud, a shower of splintered wood and leaves heralding his fall.

Seizing her chance, Shadow lunged. She aimed for his main power conduit—a strike there would end him. The world slowed as her claws found their mark, sinking into the vulnerable spot in Var's underbelly. His agonized howl echoed across the field, a primal cry.

Var's hulking form teetered before crumpling to the ground, his movements stilted. He lay there, twitching. A viscous charcoal-tinted oil dripped from his jaws.

Shadow backed away, panting heavily, her wiring

on the brink of overheating. Var had always been monstrous. Terrifying.

She hung her head. "I'm sorry." She truly was. Despite his cruelty toward her, his blind fealty to Master, he'd been following his programming.

His systems short-circuited, and sparks flickered from the gash in his belly like lightning drops against the backdrop of the battle. After a few moments, his red eyes dimmed until they extinguished.

She'd done it. Var was defeated. The Rovers were free of his dominance.

She directed her focus back to the field and the barn. *Protect the pack.* The echoes of warfare were fading. She sprinted over to Block and the others. They'd managed to drive Raze across the fence line.

"Hold your fire," Shadow said as she rushed across the clearing to get closer to Raze.

Raze kept low to the ground, snarling at Shadow. "Traitor."

Shadow ground to a halt. "He's dead. It's over, Raze."

"Liar." But Raze's ears folded back, and Shadow knew she sensed the loss.

"Leave and never cross here again." Shadow could try and fight Raze, but her victory against Var felt hollow. There had been so much death. All she wanted was for it to stop.

Raze stole a glance at the farm, as if sizing up her chances, and then retreated. Her sleek form disappeared into the foliage with a speed that belied her formidable build. Shadow knew the Rover would regroup, reassess, and possibly return. But she and her pack would handle it when it happened.

She headed toward the barn, and each step was a throb of electrical spasms. The world she'd known was gone. She was a Rover—an embodiment of Master's creation. And yet, she'd defied his directives to protect her new pack.

She'd stood against her own kind and won.

G5 passed her and patted her head. "Good." He never said a lot, but she knew he meant to praise her in his way.

Block rushed over to greet her and sank to his knees, hugging her around the neck. "I'm glad you made it, Shadow. I was so worried."

Behind him, the barn doors creaked open, revealing a sliver of warm light. Emery stood at the threshold. Her gaze met Shadow's, and a silent exchange of relief passed between them.

Emery stepped aside, allowing Shadow to pass inside. Her system hummed with exhaustion. The barn, with its familiar earthy scent, was a welcome respite. Yet, as she made her way to the corner she'd claimed as her resting spot, the eyes of her new pack— bots and humans alike—followed her.

She settled onto the cool concrete floor, her systems running diagnostic checks. Her pack was safe, for now.

A small figure approached. Block held Wally's hand. "Be very gentle," he told her.

Wally walked over to Shadow and placed her hand on the spot just behind her left ear. That was one of Shadow's favorite spots to have touched because it got itchy sometimes.

"Nice doggy," Wally said as she scratched the spot.

Shadow savored the praise. She allowed the familiar hum of the barn and the softer sounds of robots and people moving about to wash over her. She was home. This was her pack now.

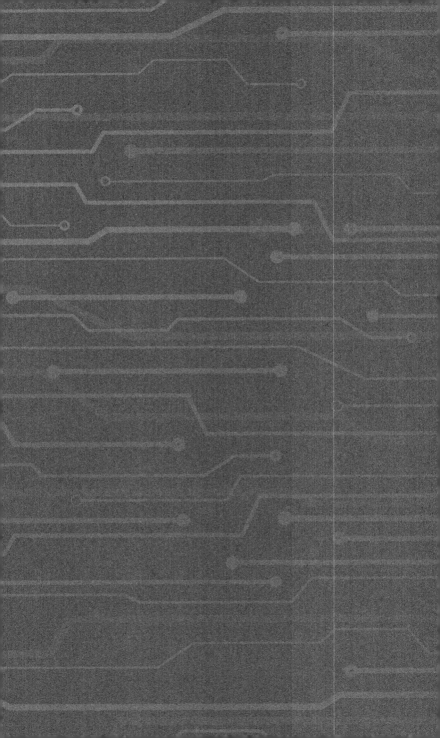

Chapter 26
We're protectors, guardians

The barn's interior was bathed in the unearthly glow of Garnet's holographic interface, casting long, wavering beams on the walls. Block had just tucked Wally into bed while Emery and Fenn caught up on some well-deserved sleep inside the house.

Forge, Maxwell, and G5 were huddled in a corner, recharging their power cells. Shadow was in standby mode as her systems repaired the damage she'd sustained. Block wasn't sure where Vacuubot was—likely patrolling the vicinity.

Block was supposed to feel something like Victory with Var defeated. Yet, the cheer that went up was punctured by the sharp reminder that Raze was still unaccounted for. That reality draped over him like a cold, damp shroud. He paced the barn floor, and his metallic feet clicked on the concrete, a steady rhythm that echoed his spiraling scenario-processing. Var was gone, but the job wasn't done. Not yet.

The others seemed not to care about the looming threat. Perhaps they reasoned that one Rover was no match for their defenses and numbers. Block stood at the barn's threshold, his sensors reaching out into the night, searching for signs of movement, an elusive silhouette, or a flicker of infrared heat.

Nothing. Raze had vanished like a fading fog.

A communication ping broke his contemplation. It was Vacuubot, dropping from twenty feet above to land on top of the goat fence. *You aren't possibly thinking of going after Raze?*

Block turned to face his friend. "Raze is still a threat. We can't sit back and wait."

You can't go out there alone, Block. We need a plan.

But Block detested each passing second. The urgency to act, to protect his home, his Wally, hung heavy around him.

"I must hunt Raze down." He was determined. It was a good time. Everyone but Vacuubot was distracted.

Vacuubot beeped and buzzed. *I'll come with you.*

But Block held his ground. "I appreciate your offer, my friend, but this is something I must do alone."

Vacuubot's hum of protest echoed against the barn's shingles. *Wait, that's nuts. You don't have to shoulder this burden alone.*

"I want to do this on my own," Block said. "My whole existence, I've been a CleanerBot. Everyone expects me to sweep the floor and get out of their way. I'm a nothing, a weakling, and I want to prove that I can do this. I can beat the Rover on my own and protect my family."

Vacuubot flew to another fencepost, closer to Block. *I get it. I was a lowly vacuum robot, the lowest of the low. But you must understand, you don't have to prove your bravery or your worth to any of us. You're a hero, and you've always been one.*

Block's sensors flickered at Vacuubot's words, a faint surge of gratitude tingling in his circuits. It was comforting to know that they saw him as more than just a CleanerBot.

"Thank you, Vacuubot. It means a lot to hear you say that." Block scanned the distant ridge of treetops visibly swaying in the breeze and lit by half a moon. "I think I need to prove it to myself."

He waited until an hour before dawn before venturing into the dense woods, his sensors meticulously searching the landscape. In the predawn gloom, each rustle and twitter of nocturnal animals magnified in the stillness. His audio receptors picked up the soft gurgling of a creek somewhere to the north, the occasional hoot of an owl, and the rustling of leaves under the cool wind.

His alloyed frame moved soundlessly, each step

measured and calculated to leave as little disturbance as possible. He traced the route Vacuubot had once showed him, relying on his memory banks to guide him through the labyrinth of trees and bushes.

The forest came alive with the first rays of sunlight, casting long shadows that danced and flickered in his visual input. The dense canopy of leaves splintered the morning light into a million shards, casting an ethereal glow on the moss-laden ground.

Every bit of information Shadow had shared about the Rovers—their habits, tracking methods, and programmed instincts swirled in his processors. His processor kept running scenarios, planning contingencies, and preparing for a confrontation that was as much inevitable as it was unpredictable.

After three hours of walking and retracing his loop, his power levels decreased noticeably. The usually steady green bar in the corner of his vision turned yellow, but it didn't stop him. He could rest later.

Each rustle in the thick underbrush sent his sensors spinning while every circuit, bolt, and gear in his body screamed for rest, but he didn't yield. His determination fueled him.

The afternoon sun settled high above. Block came to a clearing that looked upon a tranquil lake about the same size as the farm's big field. A figure sat by the water's edge.

Raze.

His threat indicator spiked, and his focus locked

onto her, analyzing, calculating. He edged closer, his steps deliberate. Quiet.

He extended the gun from inside his arm. Thanks to Garnet, his weaponry was optimized. He could take her out with a precise shot to the back of her neck.

But as his finger hovered over the trigger, he paused mid-step. Raze was hunched over, looking down into the watery surface. It was as if she studied herself.

And in that moment, Block had a profound realization—a ripple that echoed through his steel being.

Raze was trying to figure out who she was—*what* she was.

She was a Rover built for destruction. A cycle of violence, an endless loop of hostility, had defined her existence. But what if there was a different path for Raze as there was for Shadow?

The gun in his hand felt foreign now that he understood Raze. She was like him, a machine guided by programming. But Block had found a purpose beyond his initial function. Could Raze do the same?

He retracted his weapon and stepped toward her. "Raze." He kept his voice steady as she whirled around, purple eyes flashing.

"You don't need to follow Mach X anymore," he continued, his voice echoing across the still lake. "He may have created you, but you're not bound by his commands."

His sensors picked up on Raze's minimal movement, her attention focused on him.

"The farm is a haven, a safe place where we've chosen a different path. My friends, they're not soldiers, not anymore. We're protectors, guardians."

Block paused, letting his words sink in. He remembered his time at the bustling Drake hotel where he fulfilled his CleanerBot duty, unaware of the world beyond his programmed existence. His evolution had not been easy, but it had brought him purpose, companionship, and a sense of belonging. Best of all, it had brought him Wally.

"It's not your fault, you know. Mach X steered you wrong. But you can choose a different path. We can choose to be more than what we were programmed to be."

Block watched Raze. She was a creature forged from steel and circuits, cut off from her creator, and now her pack was gone. She had to be hurting. The question now was whether she would choose to be free or remain a captive of her maker's design.

"You accepted Shadow?" Raze said. "Even though she's destroyed many robots. Robots like you."

He nodded. "I can't help what Shadow did in her past, but I forgive her and welcome her. She's part of our pack now."

Raze stiffened. "That's not a true pack."

"I can't force you to change. That's a choice you must make." For the first time, Block understood what they were defending, and it was more than just a physical location. They were defending a belief in a world where they were more than just machines.

"Will you choose to join us, Raze?" He'd made his case. The decision was now hers.

Raze must've been processing his words because her optics flickered. A gentle lap of the water at the lake's edge filled the void. And then, almost imperceptibly, her rigid form softened. In that moment, Block saw the machine make a decision that defied all the programming that bound her.

"I won't return to your farm. I'll stop hunting the children. But I'm not like Shadow." Without a word, Raze turned away. Her hulking silhouette receded into the sunless woods.

Returning to the farm in the late afternoon, Block took in the pleasant scene—the barn standing tall against the blue sky, the porch of the farmhouse, and the reassuring hum of Garnet maintaining the defenses. Home.

His thoughts were a whirl of code and churning logic. His decision to confront Raze, to give her a choice, was unconventional. Dangerous. But it had been the right thing to do.

He'd thought hunting her down and killing her was the best course of action, but something in him had shifted. This wasn't merely about survival anymore. It was about living and making a stand for what he believed in.

The quiet hum of Garnet's circuits welcomed him as he stepped inside the barn. He needed to recharge and rest. He was home. Wally and the others were safe. And as he cranked down his power toward standby mode, the memory of Raze's silent retreat reassured him.

Chapter 27
The world we're fighting to create

Inside the makeshift infirmary, Nova didn't realize how heavy the SoldierBot armor had become until Cybel and Oxford finally freed her from its weight. The nanobots left tiny pin-sized holes in crisscrossing mesh patterns across her forehead, neck, arms, torso, and legs.

"That'll go away in a day or two," Cybel said.

Nova was too exhausted and aching to care as she stumbled out of the exoskeleton, relief washing over her like a crisp ocean wave. She was safely inside the Planetarium campus where they'd set up a joint Command Center comprised of the north and west factions. She barely registered the cheers that erupted outside the door, in the hallways and staging rooms, as their people celebrated the victory at the Willis Tower.

Her eyes landed on Cybel and Oxford. "You did well, Nova," Oxford said.

"Understatement of the year," Cybel added, and

Nova chuckled, wondering where she'd picked up on the phrase.

The makeshift base, situated at a strategic point in the city where they had access to boats as well as vehicles, was buzzing with activity. The hallways echoed with excited chatter. The defeat of Mach X's Chicago headquarters had sparked a new wave of hope. But as Nova pushed herself off the sickbed and looked around at the faces brimming with renewed hope and determination, she knew their fight was far from over.

"You should rest," Cybel said.

"Not now." A bone-weariness weighed on Nova as she made her way through the narrow corridors, passing by the hodgepodge of rebel fighters, technicians, and liberated bots.

Not far from her room, she found Sweep dusting cobwebs from a built-in shelf. The robot's eyes lit up. "You're up. How do you feel?"

"Meh." Nova was in no mood for small talk or pleasantries. She had work to do. Leaving unfinished business was the kind of thing that drove her crazy, even though her body was bruised, her muscles screamed in protest, and a throbbing headache was beckoning. But rest was a luxury she couldn't afford. Not yet.

Gritting her teeth, Nova headed for the main hall that functioned as an assembly space. She needed to talk to Samantha Baxter and ensure the victory they'd achieved wasn't squandered.

Samantha sat at a table with a man and woman she didn't recognize. Nova hesitated at the entrance for a moment, then walked over, doing her best to not to wince with every step.

Samantha turned, her gaze settling on Nova. A slow smile broke out as she nodded at Nova. She gestured to a wrinkled map of the city spread out on the table before them. "Come, join us." She looked at the others. "This is Nova."

The man stood. He had a sturdy build and a rugged appearance, with scars etched on his face and a thick beard that obscured his neck. He extended his hand. "Name's Ivan. I lead the far west forces around what used to be Oak Park. I heard you're the one who took out the tower. Impressive."

Nova shook his hand despite her sore muscles. "Thanks. But it was a team effort."

The woman, her blond hair tied back in a long braid, rose but kept her hands by her sides. "And I'm Sarah." Her voice was soft but steady. "I've been holding on in the South Loop. Now it's going to be easier, thanks to what you did."

Nova nodded and slid into the vacant seat next to Samantha as the others sat back down. One chair remained. "There's someone else who should be at this table."

Samantha had a sharp gaze, one that had seen the cruelties of this world and yet was lit with the stubborn flames of resilience. Samantha had been instrumental in organizing the scattered pockets of resistance. Her trust in Nova had brought many to her side, bolstering their numbers significantly. Nova had a deep respect for her, but the meeting, if they were truly planning the future for a united Chicago, was missing a crucial element.

Nova stood up and called out. "Cybel." She tilted her head at the empty chair and immediately regretted it when her neck spasmed. She gritted her teeth and hoped she didn't look as weak as she felt.

Cybel approached. "What's the matter?"

Nova pulled out the chair. "You belong here."

Cybel hesitated before sitting down, scanning the faces of the rebel leaders. Nova watched as the others welcomed her with vague nods, and she couldn't help feeling a pang of anger at their coldness. Cybel was one of the most skilled strategists she'd ever encountered, and she'd risked her life countless times for their cause. She didn't deserve to be an afterthought.

"So, let's get to business," Samantha said, pulling their attention back to the map. "Now that we've taken out—"

"Hang on," Nova interrupted. She balled her fists. "I want to take on the elephant in the room. This is Cybel Venatrix. She might be the smartest being of anyone I've ever met. She deserves a seat at the table. She speaks for the robots. Without them, we wouldn't be here. We wouldn't be celebrating a victory. Understood?"

There was a moment of silence as the rebel leaders exchanged glances, unsure of how to respond to Nova's outburst. Finally, Samantha spoke up.

"I agree," she said firmly. "We can't forget that the bots are fighting alongside us, risking their lives just as we are. They deserve a say in what happens next."

Sarah nodded, and Ivan grunted in agreement. "Fine. Cybel, you're welcome at this table," he said.

Nova relaxed her shoulders as Cybel nodded and everyone's attention focused back on the map.

After a few minutes of strategizing how to move forces about the city and divide up downtown, Nova couldn't help her frustration. "We did well at Willis Tower, but that was just one battle. The war's still on."

Sarah raised her eyebrows. "You took down the SoldierBots. We control the city now."

"Mach X is still a threat. There are more Soldier-Bots, more cities and towns enslaved, and innocent lives at stake. This is just the beginning." Nova scanning the table, meeting every gaze. "And this fight needs to be coordinated."

She continued, "We need to stand together. Organized. With a name that signifies our unity and what we stand for." She paused, letting her words sink in. "We're the Chicago Defenders."

Cybel folded her hands together. Samantha leaned back, a smile threatening to break free. Ivan's fingers tapped a slow rhythm on the table, a sign of his contemplation.

Samantha broke the silence. "Chicago Defenders . . ." she echoed. "I like it."

Nova dug a thumbnail into her left palm to hide her nerves. This was a significant step, a declaration of their identity and their mission. It was crucial that everyone agreed that the name resonated with their mission.

Cybel said, "A name to rally behind. A new start."

Ivan and Sarah didn't object. Samantha gave a single, decisive nod. "It's decided then. We're the Chicago Defenders."

Nova's aching limbs pulsed with a renewed energy. They weren't just a group of rebels anymore. They were the Defenders. Protectors of their city.

"There's something else," Nova said. "A task left to accomplish. Something I promised Samantha."

Her gaze found Samantha's. Samantha's face was unreadable, but Nova saw the flicker of anticipation in her eyes.

"Shane." The name echoed around the room like a curse, stirring up an undercurrent of old grudges and fresh betrayals. "I promised to hold a trial." Nova's voice was unwavering despite the charged silence. "A fair trial."

The others looked at Samantha. It was her twin brother Shane was accused of killing.

"He's guilty, right?" Ivan asked. "Why not just kill him?"

"He deserves a trial," Nova said. "Fairness, truth . . .

these are our pillars. This is the world we're fighting to create."

Samantha held Nova's gaze, then nodded. "Alright, Nova. We'll respect your decision."

Nova nodded. It wasn't going to be easy, but it was the right thing to do. Everyone deserved a trial.

"But," Samantha said, "we need a neutral judge. Someone who understands both sides."

Nova was already on the same track. "I have someone in mind. Doctor Emery."

"Who?" Sarah asked.

How to explain such a complicated story? Nova did her best but left out some choice parts. "She's a scientist who used to work for Mach X. She left when she realized the true nature of his plans. She's been in hiding with my friends, but she's one of the few people who didn't know Shane and can give an unbiased opinion on the matter."

"Can we trust her?" Samantha asked.

"Yes," Nova said. "She risked everything to leave Mach X. If anyone can be impartial and fair, it's her."

Nova found Geo and had him radio the farm and dispatch a truck. The trial needed to be swift.

Emery arrived the next day. Somber clouds hung over the reclaimed city. The ruins of Chicago were bathed in the early morning sunlight, casting long shadows across the debris-littered streets. Nova, in her newfound capacity as a leader of the Chicago Defenders, felt a tight knot of apprehension in her chest as she greeted Emery.

"Thanks for doing this," Nova said. She'd hoped Block would travel with her, but he must've been occupied.

Emery looked around nervously before entering the makeshift courtroom inside the glass-paned planetarium hall. "Of course," she said. "I hope I can help."

Inside, the room was tense. Shane sat in a chair with his hands cuffed on his lap. He was flanked by two armed guards. His scraggly beard was gone—they'd let him shave—and he looked a decade younger than when she'd seen him in the holding cell.

Samantha was in the front row of chairs, her expression stony. Sarah and Ivan sat in the row behind.

Nova cleared her throat. "Doctor Emery, we summoned you here to act as a neutral judge in the trial of Shane Fletcher."

Emery's gaze flickered from Shane to Nova. "I understand."

Nova continued, "Shane is accused of actions that led to the murder of Samantha's brother, Ben. This trial will determine if he's guilty or not. We ask that you listen to all sides before making a decision."

Emery nodded again and took the judge's raised seat at the front of the room. "I'll do my best to be fair and unbiased."

Samantha was to speak first. Her rigid, burning gaze locked onto Shane. The grief in her eyes was a raw, open wound. This trial was personal. "Shane got power-hungry." Her voice held firm despite the fury that shook inside her. "He informed the SoldierBots of my brother, Ben's location. Ben thought he was meeting with Shane to talk about an alliance. He ended up walking into a trap. The Bots shot him seventeen times."

Samantha's voice cracked. She steadied herself by placing her hands on the table in front of her where she stood. "He betrayed us for his ambition. And for what? Nothing was gained. My dear brother, Ben, was ripped away so young."

Emery scribbled notes on a legal pad, her expression stoic as Samantha recounted the fateful day that Ben was killed. Nova knew that Emery was taking in every detail, analyzing each word.

Shane's face remained impassive. When Samantha finished speaking, Emery turned to Shane. "Mr. Fletcher, what do you say to these allegations?"

Shane looked at Emery, then spared a glance at Nova before addressing Samantha. "I did inform the SoldierBots of Ben's location. But I never intended for him to be killed. I thought he'd be taken prisoner and used for leverage to make the west side give up their territory."

"Go on," Emery said.

Shane hesitated. "The SoldierBot in charge wanted

information on the west side rebels, and Ben would've been a valuable source. They told me they'd back off on my troops if I gave up the west. It was a mistake. I should've refused. But I was scared. Scared for my own life and those of my people."

Samantha bolted up from her seat. "Coward! You knew what Mach X was capable of. You knew you were sending Ben to his death."

Shane lowered his chin, his mouth twisted in a frown. "I was wrong. I regret it every day." He turned to Emery. "I admit my guilt. I acknowledge the pain and suffering my actions have caused. My actions took the life of Ben Baxter."

The words hung in the air. Nova swallowed, choking back a lump in her throat.

The silence was broken by Dr. Emery's measured voice, "Thank you, Shane. The court acknowledges your confession."

After a short recess, Emery delivered the verdict to the small group of witnesses. "In view of the severity of the crime committed and his admitted guilt, I find Shane guilty. His punishment is to be exiled from the city of Chicago and its outlying suburbs."

Shane lowered his head where he sat. Nova searched Samantha's face. She saw the hardness in her eyes soften, her shoulders loosened a touch. Perhaps it wasn't the punishment she'd sought, but there was a semblance of closure, a relief that justice had been served. Her brother's murderer was to be banished, erased from their lives and their city.

As Shane was led away, Nova caught up with the two guards. "Give me a moment, please."

Shane faced her with a half-smile, his hands cuffed in front of him. He was once her friend and lover, now a condemned criminal.

"Shane," she began, her voice low but firm.

He met her gaze, his eyes betraying no emotion.

"I once loved you. You were my mentor and later my partner. But you chose power over people. What you did was unforgivable."

A shadow passed over Shane's face, but he didn't break the gaze. "I'm sorry."

"Goodbye," she said.

And with that, the guards led him away. Nova turned and found Samantha waiting nearby. "You got your trial."

Samantha looked at her with a new respect in her eyes. "You kept your word."

A moment of understanding passed between them. A recognition of shared pain, regrets, and now a combined purpose. Perhaps they might even call each other friends someday, but this was just the beginning. The battle had been won, but the war was far from over. With Shane gone and new alliances forming, it was time to rebuild and prepare for what lay ahead.

Hope surged in Nova's heart. The Chicago Defenders would stand strong.

Chapter 28
Something worthy

The sun's rays warmed Block's metallic frame. Autumn had come, and he watched as Fenn and Sweep worked in tandem harvesting pumpkins, turnips, and zucchini. The task was simple, a far cry from the previous months' battle against the dangerous Rovers.

"Who would've thought," Sweep's voice carried on the breeze, "that two CleanerBots would end up as FarmBots?"

Fenn, never missing a beat, shot back, "You never know. At this rate, you might end up replacing the goats next."

Sweep paused in the middle of uprooting a pumpkin the size of her head. "Mr. Fenn, it's physically impossible for me to emulate the goats. For one thing, their bodily functions, such as producing milk—"

"I'm joking, Sweep." Fenn tipped his wide-brimmed hat back and wiped sweat from his brow.

Sweep looked at Block. She was still adjusting to being in the presence of humans and robots who acknowledged her. Humor was a new concept. Block was her mentor, teaching her about life outside the office skyscrapers she'd worked in. He found the companionship of another CleanerBot pleasant.

They'd built something valuable here. The farm, once a temporary safe haven, had transformed into their home. The echoes of children's laughter and shared meals around the broad outside dining table made every day fun. Now that the Rovers were gone and the Chicago SoldierBots had mostly been destroyed, they had time to be more relaxed.

Block looked down at his hands, once meant only for cleaning, now grabbing a yellow squash from the ground. The soil was rough, and dirtied his metal palms, but he could clean up later.

The vegetables they plucked held more than just the promise of a harvest; they symbolized their collective determination to keep moving forward. Block was where he needed to be—not just a CleanerBot but a protector, a friend, and a father. All part of something greater.

Under the warmth of the afternoon sun, Block leaned down to cut loose a particularly heavy pumpkin. Across the farmstead, the sound of laughter carried on the breeze, and he caught movement in his periphery.

Shadow was at the heart of it all. The black fur on her Rover hide glistened. She loomed over the children who ran in awkward, messy circles as they tried to keep up. Wally was strapped into a saddle on Shadow's back, her delighted giggles filling the air.

"Fly me, Shadow. Fly!" Her tiny arms were outstretched as if she was a bird rocketing through the sky.

"You're flying." The electronic hum of Shadow's words tinged with affection. "You're as swift as an eagle."

Block hoped Shadow was being careful not to go too fast. Maxwell had fashioned a small saddle from an old one in Fenn's barn. He'd made it small enough for the toddlers to use and added safety features like a seat belt. Ever since, rides on Shadow's back were all any of the kids could talk about.

Wally's laughter echoed across the field, bright and clear. Sweep stood nearby, watching the kids. "I like it here," she said.

Block had Nova to thank for finding Sweep, and from the sounds of it, she'd saved Sweep's life along with thirty or so other robots. They'd hidden in an underground train car when the EMP detonated. Afterward, the robots were given a choice as to what they wanted to do. Some decided to venture outside of Chicago and explore the country, while others volunteered to live and work the farms adjacent to Fenn's. The Chicago Defenders needed a food supply. About ten stayed behind to help Nova and the rebels recruit other robots in and around the city.

Shadow carried Wally back toward the farmhouse with the other children trailing behind them like a cheerful parade. The rumble of an engine cut through the peaceful lull, drawing Block's attention to the gravelly road leading to the house. Dust kicked up in the air, settling gradually as a blue SUV parked. Nova stepped out from the driver's side. She'd cropped her long brown hair and tucked it behind her ears. She wore jeans and a red Chicago Bulls T-shirt, more casual than he'd ever seen her look.

"Nova!" Block dropped his tools and made his way toward her. She grinned, and they embraced. Nova was safe and well.

She broke their hug and clapped him on the shoulder as she looked around at the barn and home. "You've done well here, Block." She stood back and did a double take. "What's that? Dirt on your hands?"

"Some things have changed, and thank you," he said. "It's been a team effort to get the farm in shape."

Together, they took a stroll around the property with Block pointing out the renovations and the thriving crops, and he introduced her to Garnet and Fenn.

Sweep ran up to Nova and asked politely for a hug. "Come here." Nova grabbed her and pulled her close.

Block had never seen Nova smile so much. "You've created something wonderful here, Block."

"How are things with you? Can you stay awhile? Wally would love it."

A frown crossed her features before vanishing as fast as it had come. "We're making progress. With the SoldierBots no longer a threat, the city is uniting like never before." She hesitated as if leaving something out. "Sorry, I can't stay. Where is Wally anyway?"

"Getting a ride from Shadow, much to the dismay of every other child here."

Nova halted in the field where they walked when she caught sight of Shadow. "I'll never get over the look of that robot." She shook her head. "You're sure it's safe for Wally?"

"Shadow's one of us. She and Wally have a bond." Other than Block himself, Shadow was the robot most protective of Wally.

As they walked past the vegetable garden, he told Nova about his encounter with Raze. He shared his decision to let her go, choosing empathy over violence. "It wasn't easy, but it was the right thing."

Nova nodded. "That's why you're different, Block. I think you've always been more than a CleanerBot. You're a leader. Look at how you've protected Wally all this time. And now you've given this place something that can't be programmed—a heart."

Block processed her words, turning over the magnitude of what she'd said in his logic module. Was it true? From the assembly line where he'd been crafted, to Chicago, New York, and then full circle back to an Illinois farm, he'd journeyed far from his origins. He'd learned, adapted, and fought for his and

Wally's lives. He was still a CleanerBot, and then some.

The serenity of the moment was shattered by the unmistakable roar of an engine—a deep rumbling that stoked alarm from G5 standing guard in the watchtower.

But it was a sound familiar and very dear to Block. "It's okay," he yelled to G5. A trail of dust marked the approach of the eighteen-wheeler along old Route 14. The familiar silhouette of Number 21, the autonomous semi and Block's longtime friend, came into view.

"Looks like you have more visitors." Nova's lips curved into a smile.

Block buzzed with anticipation. "It seems so." They'd returned sooner than expected.

As the truck came to a stop in the yard, its side door slid open, revealing Cybel's elegant black steel frame and Oxford's twelve-foot-tall Mech body with his bright yellow armor. He'd gotten an extensive polishing and repairs done somewhere along the way. They were finally home.

Before long, Emery, Fenn, and the curious children poured out of the barn and the farmhouse, their chatter and excitement filling the air.

Spoon, clutching a baby girl in his arms, waved enthusiastically. "Welcome back, Oxford and Cybel."

Shadow, usually guarded, had a noticeable lightness in her movements as she bowed down so Sweep could unbuckle Wally and set her on the ground. Even the typically standoffish Vacuubot hovered closer, its lights flashing in a buzzy greeting.

Block made his way toward the group, the gravel crunching under his feet. As he approached Number 21, a familiar connection pulsed in his core. "Welcome back, Twenty-one." He patted the semi's side panel.

"Good to be back, Block." 21 said.

There was laughter, stories exchanged, and a sense of relief from the traveling robots.

"Let's eat," Emery said after a while. She kept the kids on a routine eating schedule to keep their moods in check.

As dusk settled, a soft golden light from the barn spilled across the large picnic table set in the yard. Block, Nova, and the others gathered around, watching as the children tucked into a well-deserved dinner.

Cybel and Oxford, now dust-free and powered up, held court at one end of the table. The children were remarkably quiet as they stared at Oxford's tall form. They'd never seen a robot so massive. Block, seated next to Nova, found himself hanging on every word.

"The east is different than what we expected," Cybel said. "Mach X's grip is not as tight as it used to be."

Block's focus sharpened. "What do you mean?"

"The SoldierBots are dwindling," Oxford said. "It appears that a new faction of robots has risen. They're not like us, but they're also not under Mach X's control."

Vacuubot buzzed overhead, its sensors glowing brighter.

"Are they allies?" Nova asked.

"We don't know yet," Cybel admitted. "They seem to have their own agenda. But they've been causing trouble for Mach X's forces."

Nova leaned in, her gaze intense. "This could be a game-changer."

"Yes," Cybel agreed. "But we need to tread carefully. Not all who oppose Mach X are friends."

Emery had been silent until then, chewing her food and listening with care. She spoke up. "He's damaged or dead. If he hasn't attempted contact with Shadow, and the SoldierBots are faltering, it has to mean he's beyond repair."

"I wish we knew for sure," Nova said.

The conversation ebbed and flowed, their speculations and strategies weaving a tapestry of possibilities. Yet amid the uncertainty, the news from the east brought them a sense of hope. Their stand against Mach X had not been in vain.

Block looked around at his chosen family—Nova's cheeks lit by the warm glow from candles, Wally asleep in his arms, Shadow's muzzle nestled against his foot. Despite the challenges that lay ahead, there was a sense of peace. Being together meant everything. Unity was their most potent weapon.

"We have to try and ally with the rebel bots in the

east," Cybel said. The silence that followed hung heavy in the air.

She's right. Vacuubot messaged Block. *Cybel usually is.*

Nova spoke first. "If there's a chance this new faction could help us make sure Mach X and his SoldierBots are destroyed, we should explore it."

Oxford nodded. "It won't be easy. And there's a risk, as always. We'll back you up."

Block's optical sensors stayed fixed on Nova. There was worry etched into his processor's logic circuits, but he understood the weight of Nova's drive to form an alliance. He'd seen her brave dangerous situations countless times before.

"I know." Nova's voice was firm. "But it's a risk I'm willing to take. For us, for the children, and"—she looked at Sweep—"for all the robots still chained under Mach X's control."

There was a collective hum of agreement around the table. Under the table, Nova patted Block's hand. Despite her fears, she was ready to take on a daunting task for the greater good. It was what made her who she was—a leader.

Number 21 flashed his headlights from thirty feet away where he sat parked. "I couldn't help but eavesdrop. If it's east you're heading, Nova, I'll get you there."

The reality of the situation sank in for Block. Nova was about to embark on another stride toward freedom.

But this time, the battlefield was much larger, and the future—if they won—was brighter than it had ever been.

In the deepening twilight, Emery announced a diversion. She unfolded a set of paper lanterns she'd been saving for a special occasion. Wally and the kids gathered around her, their eyes wide with excitement as she explained the process.

"We're going to write down our wishes, and then we'll set these lanterns into the sky." Emery handed out crayons and scraps of paper. "Kids, draw a picture."

Wally was the first to doodle her wish. She sat in Emery's lap as she scrawled onto the rough paper. "Shadow and Daddy," she declared and tossed her crayon away. Her rendering of Block and Shadow was a cartoonish sketch of two stick figures that made Emery chuckle and Shadow wag her tail.

One by one, they each drew out or wrote down their wishes. Block watched, a gentle heat coursing through his circuits as he took in the scene. When it was his turn, he carefully took the pen in his metallic grip. The words came to him easily. "For the continued strength and protection of our family," he wrote.

They ignited the lanterns one by one, their soft light illuminating the faces of the unconventional gathering. The robots, adults, and kids watched in silence as the lanterns floated higher, their glowing forms receding into the darkness.

They watched until the last lantern was a mere

speck in the night. Block knew their journey was far from over, and the path ahead contained unknown dangers. But standing under the starlit sky, watching their wishes fly to the heavens, he knew they were ready to face whatever lay ahead.

The farmstead, bathed in moonlight, was peaceful. The chatter that had filled the evening was replaced by the tranquil sounds of the night—the rustling leaves, the distant hoot of an owl, the soft snores of the five sleeping toddlers who had curled up on a blanket next to Shadow.

Block scanned the familiar faces around the table. There was Dr. Emery, her face softened by the moonlight, eyes sparkling with a rare peace as she sipped a glass of merlot that Fenn had retrieved from his cellar. Wally, fast asleep against Shadow's neck, the remnants of her wide grin still present even in slumber. Shadow's mechanical tail softly swaying as she kept a vigil over the children. Cybel, Oxford, Fenn, Maxwell, Forge and Vacuubot, each caught in conversations or lost in their own logic processing.

And then there was Sweep, who'd found a new purpose in farm life. She'd seamlessly integrated into their newfound family and was a welcome addition.

Each of them had their unique stories and individual paths that had led them to this night. And now they were a part of something larger. Something *worthy*. They were no longer just bots on the run or a disconnected group of survivors. They were a family—a pack.

As he settled into his nook inside the barn and powered into standby mode for the night, Block's final thought for the night was simple. *We are a pack, and this is our home. Tomorrow, we build our future.*

Block's story continues . . .

Dear Reader,

Thanks for reading the *Rusted Wasteland* series! The next book in the series is *Steel Legacy*.

Have you read Block's journal logs from Chicago? You'll discover what happened in the days before the Uprising and how the aftermath affected him and others at the hotel.

You can download *STEEL APOCALYPSE* (*A Robot's Journal*) for free by visiting: CameronCoral.com/Block Journal

Enjoy,

Cameron Coral

P.S. - Did you enjoy this book? I'd love a review wherever you purchased this book if you have a few minutes. Thank you kindly because reviews mean a lot to me. They show me you want me to keep writing, and they help other readers discover my books.

Also by Cameron Coral

Rusted Wasteland Series:

STEEL GUARDIAN

STEEL DEFENDER

STEEL PROTECTOR

STEEL SIEGE

STEEL SOLDIER

STEEL LEGACY

STEEL APOCALYPSE (*A Robot's Journal*) - get it for free on
cameroncoral.com/blockjournal

Cyborg Guardian Chronicles:

STOLEN FUTURE

CODED RED

ORIGIN LOOP

Rogue Spark Series:

ALTERED

BRINK

DORMANT

SALVAGE

AFTER WE FALL (*A Rogue Spark Novel*) - get it for free on
CameronCoral.com

Short Stories:

CROSSING THE VOID: A Space Opera Science-Fiction Short Story

Author's Note

Dear Reader,

I'm excited to bring you Steel Soldier! Book 5 was a blast to write, especially the new character POV of Shadow, the Rover with a conscience. She's a character inspired by the adoption of my "shorty" Jack Russell terrier, Marty. Having a dog has shown me how intelligent, loving, and wonderful they are. If you subscribe to my newsletter, you'll often see pictures of her. She's my writing assistant, always by my side as I create new worlds and characters. (Newsletter sign up at: CameronCoral.com)

I also drew upon the mechanical hound from Ray Bradbury's Fahrenheit 451 and an episode of Black Mirror where people are hunted by robot dogs (pretty scary).

Author's Note

The world's technology is changing rapidly around us. When I started writing about Block's adventures in 2019, I never would've imagined that the advances in AI would be so rapid and revolutionary. It's certainly an exciting time to be alive.

Despite the post-apocalyptic setting, my writing will (I hope) show my optimism about AI's future. There are many more adventures to come in the Rusted Wasteland world, so please stick around and keep reading!

Cameron Coral
Illinois, August 2023

About the Author

Cameron Coral is an award-nominated science fiction author. Her book *Steel Guardian* about a post-apocalyptic CleanerBot placed second in the Self-Published Science Fiction Competition (SPSFC).

Growing up with a NASA engineer in the family instilled a deep respect for science and for asking lots of questions. Watching tons of Star Trek episodes helped, too. Her imagination is fueled by breakthroughs in robotics, space travel, and psychology.

After moving around a lot (Canada, Arizona, Maryland, Australia), she now lives in Northern Illinois with her husband and a "shorty" Jack Russell terrier who runs the house.

Want a free novel, advance copies of books, and occasional rants about why robots are awesome? Visit her website:
CameronCoral.com

Printed in Great Britain
by Amazon